SUBMITTING TO THE ALIEN BARBARIAN

PETRA PALERNO'S FILTHY SHORTS
BOOK 1

PETRA PALERNO

SUBMITTING TO THE ALIEN BARBARIAN

PETRA PALERNO'S FILTHY SHORTS

For those of us who want to be thrown around by a giant barbarian alien.

CONTENTS

PETRA PALERNO'S FILTHY SHORTS

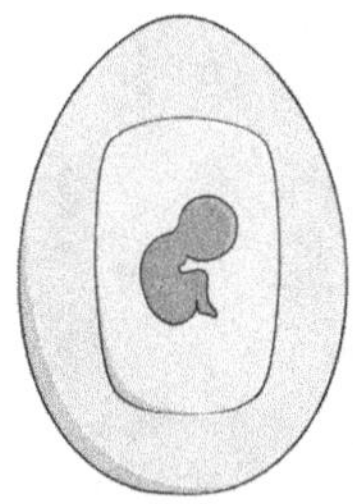

Signing up for an alien breeding program should be scary, considering the aliens are ruthless barbarians. On the upside, they won't hesitate to give it to you as rough as you like it.

Submitting to the Alien Barbarian is part of a smutty novella collection, Petra Palerno's Filthy Shorts, that features otherworldly love interests.

In this installment, you'll find: alien romance, size difference, double dongs, submission, bratting, breeding, will it fit, rough play and pregnancy.

TRIGGER AND CONTENT WARNINGS

These erotic short stories are great for a quick, smutty, read. Please mind the triggers though, as these shorts may vary wildly in content and tone from the novels I've released previously.

Remember your mental health matters.

TW/CW: rough consensual sex, primal play, knotting, breeding, aliens, dominance/submission, blood play, spanking, pregnancy, fisting, overstimulation, anal play, gagging, violence, birthing, science fiction medical procedures and murder.

CHAPTER ONE

The heat radiating from the crowd, along with the smell of sex, hits me in the face as the door clicks open and the pilot bot dumps me unceremoniously into the dirt.

My heart thuds in my chest, but it's not the excitement I thought I would feel.

I'm scared shitless.

But this is what I wanted, this is what I signed up for.

"Mates needed for Volkroth spawning season. Generous payment and all expenses paid for biologically compatible species."

You wanted someone to be rough with you, to be a fucking barbarian with you.

Maybe it was too much to expect an orientation before being dropped off at the spawning pits. I figured after the extensive medical testing to ensure biological compatibility, they'd ease me in.

I was so wrong.

Besides the chorus of fucking masses that surround me, there's the guttural noises of males as they slam their fists into each other's bodies. The spawning pit seems like it's half a sparring one.

Something I didn't realize from the holo communication is that the aliens are fucking huge. They tower over me as one purple brute rips the other male off a yellow alien female, who arguably looks like she's having a great time. She even laughs as the male turns and clocks the attacking alien on the jaw.

His bones snap, sounding like a lightning-struck tree, as he crumples to the ground. I'm not sure if the breaking noise was his jaw or his neck—but I don't think any of the warlord aliens care.

They're barbaric! They kill soldiers deemed too weak to fight. How could you want to mate a Volkroth? My roommate's disgusted face flashes in my mind as I wonder if the alien on the ground is dead or not.

I'm really here, and despite it being what I want, I'm scared. At no point did I think it would be like what I'm seeing now. I can't tear my eyes away from the blood that streams from the fallen alien's ear.

He's dead.

"If you're too weak to fight, you're too weak to carry on the bloodline," the victor yells before grabbing the yellow alien female and slinging her over his shoulder. She laughs as the male smacks her ass and drags her off somewhere to breed.

I gulp, my throat dry, and try once again to get my bearings. Despite the frenzied brawling and fucking, there's a very clear division of who is actually being attacked. The Volkorth fists only connect with the other males around them.

"Sofuckinggood!" A gray skinned female moans before a male with a broken horn grabs her neck. Her eyes roll into the back of her head as she comes, his hips slamming hers into the dirt.

I want that, I want to be used, I want these barbarians to fuck me. Despite the fear that courses through my veins, there's something hot about the idea that I could be in danger. My hand drifts to my ear at the thought, the metal cuff now there as a tracking device. It's linked to my vitals in a way where the overseers would know if something goes wrong. A safety precaution for someone looking to be unsafe.

There are raucous roars behind me, and my attention snaps to a transport unit as a group of what looks like fresh breeding males jump from the open cargo bay. I hold my breath, waiting to get trampled or thrown over someone's brawny shoulder. They all rush for the writhing madness of the pit, a herd of muscled bodies, save for one.

As the red dust settles, I see him looking—no, more like staring—at me. The male's physique looks as though he's been carved from purple marble. His is body slick and shining, and unlike the one I saw on the holo comm, he's completely nude.

More importantly, the big beast has two massive cocks resting on one heavy set of balls. They twist around each other, almost looking like they're prehensile. I must gasp, because he arches a black brow.

I scramble to stand when the alien's eyes fall on me. His thick black hair, falling free of his topknot, spills over the four horns. There are two on either side of his head that curl proudly away from his face, and a shorter set between those.

"A human?" He almost laughs as he says it. "I'd have thought your kind too soft, too exotic to be in the spawning pits with the rest of us."

His voice is deadly smooth as he approaches me, a predator stalking his prey. Could I even hear his footsteps on this crimson earth if not for the pounding of my heartbeat in my ears?

I freeze, even though my brain is screaming to flee, that I shouldn't let this monster near me.

But there's a broken part of my judgement that wants him to grab me by the neck and fuck me into the dirt. So I stay still, a prisoner between my two desires, my heart in my throat.

I crane my head up to look at him now that he's so close. He moves one very deliberate step ever nearer. I can feel his breath on my face.

His eyes darken, and he licks his lips.

"You should run." His voice is almost a whisper as it leaves his mouth.

As my adrenaline kicks in, the logical part of my mind wins, and I bolt. But I don't have time to worry about where I'm running to. His huge hand shoots around my midsection, pulling me back against his body.

Two enormous cocks strain against my ass, the thin fabric of my jumpsuit doing nothing to protect me from the heat of his body. He brings his free hand up to my neck and squeezes rough fingers against the column of my throat. It sends sparks down to my weeping pussy, and I squirm in his hold.

"I want you full and dripping with my seed, and *only mine*, human," he breathes into my ear.

I bite back a moan.

"That's why you're here, isn't it? You want a beast to breed you, to make you submit?"

"Yes," I manage to eek out. The first words I've spoken on this planet are to agree to be some space barbarian's plaything.

The alien rips the neckline of my jumpsuit, exposing my breast to the planet's humid air. My nipples pebble instantly as he drags his calloused hand over my sensitive flesh.

The hand on my neck weaves into my hair, grabbing my ponytail and yanking my head further back until my cheek rests against his. His stubble rubs my cheek raw.

"How do you want it?" he asks.

"Rough," I groan as his fingers pinch my nipple. I arch my back, searching for some friction as my hips lift. I want him to fuck me.

Suddenly, there's a flash of pain and I yelp as his hand comes down hard, sharply smacking my tit.

"Can you handle rough, with all this softness?" His palms smooth over the agitated skin of my red breast, the stinging melting into something blurred with an intense pleasure.

"Only one way to find out," I say, with some shocking boldness. "Fuck me."

His breath catches at my change in tone.

The fear has flown from my body. From that first slap, I know that this is what I want. I have no desire to keep begging my partners to go harder or deeper. The thought of causing someone to feel ashamed of me by asking them to slap me across my face is soul crushing. I need whoever I'm fucking to want to do it as much as I want it done to me. My body sings with joy. I want him to use me, to fucking breed me.

I look back at the alien, and his brows knit. A look of resolution crosses his face.

"I won't share you," he says as his arm wraps around my waist, and he throws me roughly over his shoulder.

CHAPTER TWO

"Hey, where are we going?" I pound my hand against his back. "You're supposed to fuck me!" I grumble like a petulant child as he trots away from the wild revelry happening behind us.

"Somewhere I can take my time with you, human."

"Fuck you!" I slam my fist into his back. "I said fuck me!"

I don't want to be taken somewhere else, I want to join the orgy.

He doesn't listen, so I do the only thing I can think to get him to stop. I turn my head, taking his flesh between my lips. My teeth find the shell of his ear, and I bite down hard until I taste the coppery tang of blood.

He stumbles and pries me off his ear with rough hands and throws me flat onto my back. The red dirt swirls around me in the air. I lick his blood off my lip, staring directly into the barbarian's soul.

I barely have time to catch my breath before thick hands grab me by my hips and flip me over, forcing the side of my face into the ground.

"Is this what you want?" he yells, ripping what's

left of the jumpsuit off my ass. "You want me to fill up your human cunt with my warrior's seed?"

One of his hands finds the slickness between my thighs, while the other pushes my head harder against the ground. The entwined cocks I see out of my peripheral vision seem even bigger this close.

His thick finger thrusts hard into me, stretching my entrance before he adds another and pounds even deeper yet. My pussy clamps over his calloused fingers, and I swear I'm almost ready to come just from his hand.

"Could you even take my cocks in this tiny human cunt of yours?" he asks as he moves his hand back to his own pulsating members.

The loss of him has my pussy clenching over nothing, the ache in my core almost unbearable.

"Make it fit, you coward," I tell him. I can't wait any more for release. I need this.

His hand leaves my head, and I turn to get a better look at his face. His throbbing cocks are notched at my entrance. Those eyes shine with some kind of viciousness I've only dreamed about, and something behind his visage snaps. His nostrils flare, and the time for talking is done.

I swear the planet stops its spinning in orbit for a moment, and every part of my spirit is tautly strung.

"Use me," I whisper.

He plunges into me, and it fucking burns. He doesn't ask if I'm okay, he doesn't allow me time to adjust, he just keeps up his relentless rhythm. The pain and pleasure mix in a way I've never experienced before, and I make noises that sound more animal than human.

The coil of his cocks hit my G-spot with every thrust, and despite the pain there's a tension as an orgasm builds with a hungry intensity. My body wants this, it yearns to submit.

"You'll come on my cocks and then milk me so hard that you'll be dripping my seed for weeks. Your used cunt will belong only to me. You're going to be marked forever in my cum. No one will dare touch you ever again. I'm going to fuck you raw," the Volkroth bellows, his words coming faster as his pace increases.

When he puts his hand back on my throat, squeezing the sides hard, and my vision narrows. For a split second, I know nothing but him. The sensation of his fingers digging into my skin, his cocks drilling deeply, and every single nerve in my body readying itself for release. When the taut cord inside me finally snaps, waves of ecstasy replace any lingering pain. My body throbs with pleasure from my toes to the top of my head, every muscle seizing in a symphony of joy.

In my boneless haze, I feel his body tighten. Inside me, his massive cocks move and unfurl as if they're rearranging themselves. I throb as they do, even though I'm spent. My oversensitive flesh can barely handle the sensation before I feel something swelling inside me.

I look up as some realization sparks behind the alien's eyes. Something isn't right. He almost looks as though he wants to pull out, but even in my stupor, I know he's too far gone. His hips jerk and he lets out the most ragged of breaths as he presses on the bulge he's created in my stomach as he comes. His hot seed washes over my insides, stoppered up by his swollen shafts.

He's still coming when it begins to leak out and down my thighs. My clasping walls grip onto him, and I feel locked together.

Eventually, the giant collapses on top of me,

even though I expect him to head back to the crowd.

"What are you doing?" I ask.

"You don't know what you've done, do you?" He's out of breath, and he sounds shocked. He blinks a few times and scrubs a hand over his face. Putting a hand on the ground, he attempts to withdraw from my pussy. He groans, something between pleasure and disbelief. "I've knotted inside you, we're stuck like this until the swelling goes down."

I flex my inner walls, and I can feel the bulge of his twisted cocks locking us together. This isn't something they went over in my orientation. Even though his body is still, his members continue to pump hot semen deep inside of me.

"If you keep doing that with your cunt, we'll be here forever, human," he growls.

Wrapping an arm around my back, he pulls me against his body, my head barely reaching his pecs, and flips over so that I'm lying on his chest.

"So, what happens after this?" I ask, feeling like my body has not a single bone left to keep me steady. I catch myself rubbing my face in his thick chest hair, totally blissed-out after our experience together.

"I do it again, and again, until I'm sure my seed takes and your belly is swollen. I'll fuck your human cunt as many times as it takes to ensure my bloodline," he says as if it's the only obvious choice.

"If I let you," I whisper snarkily.

White flashes behind my eyes as his hand smacks my ass.

"You'll do as you're told," he says before closing his eyes and ignoring me.

And I will. I'll do whatever he asks if he keeps making me feel like this.

CHAPTER THREE

I'm barely awake when his cocks loosen and slide out of my dripping pussy.

I don't know how I'm supposed to keep going after that. I'm sore and stinging, drenched in a strange alien's cum. This is precisely what I wanted...but I'm not sure if I can rally for a round two with some other barbarian.

Especially not after that "knot" stretched me as wide as it did.

I expect the big purple brute to roll me off to the side and continue his revelry back with the rest of the female aliens I saw back at the pit.

But he doesn't. He takes my used body and tucks me into his arms, carrying me like a limp doll. I blink rapidly, trying to clear the red dirt from my eyes. The particulates sting, and my eyes water, trying to clear the offending matter.

Staring up at his beard-covered square jaw, I realize that he's once again walking away from the crush of the crowd.

"Hey," I cough out. "Where are you taking me? Shouldn't I go forth and spawn?" My voice is hoarse as I poke his muscular side. Was I screaming when he fucked me before? Is that why my throat feels so rough?

He stops walking and tilts his head down with a look of disgust.

"You. Took. My. Knot," he seethes through gritted teeth. "Don't think for a second I'm allowing you to sully yourself with another Volkroth's seed. Did I damage your brain when I slammed it into the ground?" He puffs a quick burst of air through his nostrils, pulling me closer to him.

"Hey, fuck you," I rasp. "Where the fuck are we going, then?" Though I realize if he wants to take me somewhere, he will—and I won't be able to stop him.

"Homecave," he grunts. "Stop asking so many questions, human. I'm tired of talking."

"Well, you picked the wrong gal then, because talking shit is probably the only thing I'm good at."

"If you don't shut your mouth, I'll gag you," he says plainly.

"Is that a promise?" I grin up at him, despite my aching body.

He looks down at me in his arms and cocks a brow. Without giving me an answer, he sets me on the ground. My legs shake, still unstable from his ministrations earlier.

He gazes over the exposed lower half of my body. I've got nothing on by the bits of ripped jumpsuit left hanging from me. With a smile on his face, the alien reaches out and grabs hold of the tattered remains of my pant leg, which is still wrapped around my ankle. The remaining fabric flutters in the wind behind me.

As he forcefully tears it off, my leg buckles and I collapse onto one knee. With swift movements, he ties a tight knot at the center of the strip.

Leaning over, he clutches my face with his powerful hand, digging his fingers into my cheeks.

"Open your mouth, human," he growls.

"Make me," I say with lips as closed as I can make them.

Despite his scowl, he pries open my mouth with ease, his finger slipping between my teeth. His hand still carries the lingering taste of me. No matter how hard I try, his superior strength renders my attempts to bite him futile, leaving my jaw barely able to move.

With his other hand, he pushes the knot between my teeth and pulls the ends of the fabric tight around the back of my head.

As he runs his finger over my cheek, he whispers, "I like you better this way," before swiftly lifting my body onto his shoulder.

With each yell into his back, spit accumulates around the gag, making it increasingly uncomfortable. The fabric's rough edges dig into the corners of my mouth, intensifying the struggle.

No matter how hard I attempt to outdo this imposing barbarian, he matches my bratting blow for blow—and I fucking love it.

As I squirm over his shoulder, he tightens his grip on my ankles, nails digging into my flesh. His other hand runs up and down my exposed ass, stroking it in a way that feels too soft for his calloused hand. His palm creeps closer to my pussy but never touches it. The denial of his touch makes it weep slickness, but I don't know if he can tell the difference between my arousal and his cum

I don't think he cares either way.

There's some shuffling, and he pushes what seems like a leather hide aside as we step through a stone opening. I think we're in a cave. It's dimly lit and humid wherever we are. I swear I can hear him softly humming, as if he's quite pleased with himself.

He sets me down roughly in front of a central fire, the smoke stinging my already agitated eyes. It takes a moment to feel the soft fur beneath me.

I look down at the thick yellow pelt, saliva running down my chin as I tilt my head. It feels strange to be placed on something so soft, the feeling so out of place in this rough world I've volunteered to be a part of.

I drag my eyes up, adjusting to the lighting of the cave. The walls are covered in more hides in unusual colors. Crudely built shelves hold supplies.

Water gurgles softly behind me.

I whip my head around to see the rear of the cave open up to some kind of bubbling hot spring. It smells slightly of sulfur and reminds me of the well water I grew up drinking.

I hear the alien's footsteps and face forward. He stands on the other side of the fire. The light from the flames highlights the sheen of sweat over his chiseled form. He looks at me with hooded lids. His possessiveness is as plain as day.

"I'll remove the gag if you can behave. Speak when spoken to," he says calmly.

I nod, unsure if I can keep that promise, but excited to find out what will happen if I don't.

He steps around the fire and releases the fabric knot from the base of my skull.

The soaked gag drops to the ground, and I rub the corners of my mouth and flex my tongue out.

He pants, his exhalations fanning over me, as if waiting for my snarky response.

"What?" I ask. For someone who doesn't want me to talk, he sure looks like he's expecting me to.

"Do you have a question?" he snaps.

"Sure, do you have a name?" I don't know what to call him other than asshole.

"Drohako."

His name suits him, and I mouth it a few times before I get comfortable with the pronunciation.

He sits down next to me, crossing his legs and letting his monster cocks unfurl as he relaxes. He catches me gazing back at him expectantly.

"What?" he says, annoyed.

"So, Drohako, do you want to know my name?" I ask, already assuming the answer is yes.

"Hush," he murmurs, cutting off my words. He wraps his arm around me and guides us both down to rest on the cozy furs.

CHAPTER FOUR

I reach for him but find nothing but a fistful of yellow fur. Maybe he's finally gone back to the orgy and found something else to rut.

I blink, trying to clear my crusted eyes of sleep. Could I even find my way back to the spawning pits on my own? I wasn't really paying attention to what direction he walked when I was slung over his shoulder.

He couldn't have walked that far, could he?

With a deep breath, I push my body up to sit; every muscle feels overworked and stiff. Bringing my hands down to my pussy, I wince.

Being overworked is an understatement. I'm ninety-nine percent sure that I've torn something.

Sure, I like it rough, but everyone's got a limit. I could stay here one more night and soldier back to the pits for more fun before I'm taken to the Volkroth nesting grounds.

The actual giving birth part of the breeding program isn't really the thing that excites me, but it's kind of a package deal. Luckily, I've been assured that the gestation time is short and birth is much easier than for normal humans. The Volkroth deliver very undeveloped young, and they are brought to term outside the body at the nesting grounds.

When it was being described to me, they made it seem like they reproduced similarly to pandas or kangaroos—but no pouch was required. The tiny baby bean goes into some kind of pod, and I can go about getting fucked roughly for the rest of the spawning season. The Volkroth males raise the young communally too, so there's no expectation of parenting for me, either.

Looking at the sheer size of the Volkroth, the whole idea of a tiny bean of a baby seems ludicrous. But then again, I'm no expert on alien reproduction.

I'm just here to be ripped apart, and I've still got three months left until the spawning season ends. One rest day won't put that big a damper on my orgy fun, will it?

The fire I slept next to is low, and I nudge a puck of the fuel I saw Drohako stoke it with last night into the flames. They instantaneously spark and the fire greedily engulfs the puck of dried vegetation and mud.

I'm just about to lie back down when I hear grunting and the hide that covers the cave entrance flies open.

The sun blasts into the cave, and my eyes struggle to adjust to the alien sun's intensity. Slowly, two forms block out the light.

Drohako stands, one arm up, holding the lead to some huge alien animal. As he guides it through the opening, it limps on one of its four legs.

"Stupid Grasyi, I hope the run was worth it," he barks at the beast that looks like a cross between a Bengal tiger and a moose.

As he ties the animal up, I see its legs are far too tall to belong to a big cat, but its blocky head is feline. A set of large and branching black antlers curl around its head. Its bright yellow fur is thick and fluffy, but I can tell it masks how vicious the beast is. The animal's almond eyes flick over to me as it licks its lips lazily, revealing a viciously sharp set of teeth.

"Drohako?"

"Who else would it be?" He turns to me, annoyed and scowling.

"I don't know. I figured you headed back to the spawning pits. Don't get pissy with me." I stand slowly and with a great deal of shaking effort.

"And now you're hurt, too? You, little human, might have eyes bigger than your cunt." He gestures down to his crotch. Some kind of loincloth covers his massive cocks. It does little to hide his thunder, so to speak.

I scoff, but he's probably not wrong. Taking a step forward, my knees unexpectedly give out. Closing my eyes, I expect to fall face first into the fire.

I feel the heat on my cheeks but not the licking sting of the flames. Bringing my hand up to my chest, I feel Drohako's brawny forearm. It grips my chest tightly, holding me just above the fire.

"You move pretty fast for a big guy," I chirp, still woozy.

"You are injured," he tells me earnestly.

"No shit, Sherlock," I mutter under my breath, and he pulls me into his arms.

"You will tell me next time you're injured. You won't be stupid like this again," he scolds as we walk further into the cave.

My stomach grumbles and clenches uncomfortably. "Maybe I'm just hungry."

Drohako groans. "You are both, and you've informed me of neither."

"Sorry, I thought you hit it and quit it," I laugh. "I'm sure I would have figured it out once I made it back to the spawning pits—"

Drohako wraps his hand around my hair and tugs my head back hard.

"You are not going back to the spawning pits. In fact, you will not leave the homecave," he seethes.

"What? Were you serious last night? Isn't that the point of me being here?" He steps over some kind of ledge, and I realize he's lowering us both into the hot spring I saw last night.

Drohako tucks his legs under him, sitting over his crossed ankles, and cradles me as he slowly brings my body under the water's surface. Now that I'm actually in it, I don't think it's water. It's not sticky, but it is thick like syrup. It clings to my body and displaces in ways that water wouldn't. As I lie across his lap, he looks at me with a sour scowl and tugs my hair back into the pool.

"Hold your breath."

I don't do it fast enough, and some water gets into my nose and lungs. I choke when he lets me up, gasping for air and forcing the warm water out of my chest.

"What the fuck? You're mad that I'm injured, so you try to drown me?" I sputter.

"The frustrating fact that you have no self-preservation skills and also can't follow instructions isn't my fault...now is it? Quit complaining before I gag you again. The planet's blood is healing." He acts like he would rather do anything other than caring for me...but does it all the same.

"Planet's blood? Healing?" I ask, but realize that he's right. My muscles are relaxing, and even my crotch isn't as sore.

"How injured is your cunt?" he asks as if we're talking about the weather.

"It's sore," I say, trying to mitigate how painful it actually is.

With a sigh and an eye roll, he spins me so that my head rests just below his pecs. I feel pint-sized when he's manhandling me.

I don't resist when he pulls my knees apart wide enough so that my feet fall on the outside of his own legs. I watch him with curiosity as he slides a big purple hand between my legs. He rubs broadly over my mound and lips, working the healing water over my pussy.

I ease into him as some of the stinging is instantly soothed.

My mouth parts as his hand dips lower, and two of his thick fingers run up and down the lips of my pussy before pressing into my entrance. I flinch slightly as he touches my torn skin.

"I should fuck you even rawer for not telling me you were hurt," he says through gritted teeth.

I wonder if maybe he actually did scramble something in my brain when he slammed it into the ground. A cord tightens inside me as my arousal grows. It would fucking hurt, but in a way I feel I would like.

I buck my hips a little, maybe giving him the gentle nudge he needs to fucking wreck me again.

His other hand wraps around my neck, squeezing the sides hard. I bite my lip, unable to help the warmth spreading over my body.

"You are an insolent thing who will only get fucked once she listens. You're going to have to earn these cocks."

I expect him to move his hands a little faster, perhaps slipping at least one of his cocks up into me.

But he doesn't. He rubs my torn pussy slowly, and I can almost feel it mending itself, thanks to the weird alien liquid. The new skin that grows is more sensitive than what was there before, and it doesn't lessen my arousal.

"Do you want this seed filling your belly, growing my spawn?" He breathes into my ear, and all the while, his hands move torturously slow on my no longer painful pussy.

"Yes," I sigh as he squeezes my neck all the harder.

"Do you want your tight little human cunt to milk these cocks?" he rasps, letting his fingers find my clit. Because the liquid we're in, the planet's blood, is thick and viscous, it lets him glide over the sensitive spot at my pussy's apex with ease.

My legs shake as he runs circles around the bundle of nerves, my muscles clasping, begging to be filled up with his thick cocks. I want to feel the delicious swell of his knotting dicks again.

"Please, Drohako," I moan, arching up.

"Do you want to come, little human?" He bites my earlobe hard.

"Fuck yes," I say, so close to the edge of no return.

"Then you will fucking listen to me from now on." His tone changes from sensual to angry in the span of a heartbeat.

I'm surprised when he stops petting my pussy and pushes my knees shut. I'm still throbbing with need when he pushes me forward into the pool so he can leave it.

"Did you really just do that?" I pant as he walks back toward the front of the cave, pushing my own hand between my thighs. If I don't find my release, I feel like I'll explode, and my fingers work furiously, trying to expedite my own ecstasy.

"Don't you fucking dare touch yourself," his voice booms as he snarls at me. I jump almost as much as the strange creature tied up by the cave's entrance. "You will come only when I allow it, and right now, you don't deserve it."

Oh. This is a thing, a thing I like. *Do I get off on withholding?*

"You will let your body heal, you will eat the food I'm about to bring you, and you will stop talking about returning to the spawning pits. You took my knot, you are my mate." He balls up his fists. "I will teach you some godsdamn discipline if it's the last fucking thing I do." His purple face is flushed near blue as he points an accusatory finger at me.

"Your mate?" I ask, bewildered.

CHAPTER FIVE

I pull myself out of the water and sit down, dripping wet, on the furs near the fire. "What do you mean that I'm your mate? Isn't the whole point of Volkroth spawning season is that there are no mates. I was under the impression it was a kind of 'free use' scenario around here."

He's got to be joking, right?

Drohako sets his jaw, but his eyes soften from the blind rage of earlier. His gold irises bore into my soul as he speaks.

"I can see that you weren't aware of every possibility here," he sighs, scrubbing a hand over his face.

"Obviously," I say with a roll of my eyes. "What exactly did I get myself into?"

Despite trying to play it cool, I'm nervous as hell about what he might say.

"It is common for my people to breed only in the spawning pits. As I'm sure the representative informed you, the Volkroth only produce male offspring. We've needed females from other species for longer than I've existed. The Volkroth have adapted to this way of life—but it's not how it's always been." He seems to have calmed down a little as he sits next to me. His meaty thighs fold under him as he does.

"I knew you, this unassuming, aggravating little thing, were my mate the second you took the thick knot of my cocks. That isn't something that happens every time we rut a female, human." His voice deepens as he talks about being buried inside me.

"Mate... The aliens on the station have those. Are you telling me we're like...married now?" My throat gets sticky and the word marriage feels thick, like peanut butter.

"I do not know what this marriage word means —if it means that you are mine, and then I will pump you full of my seed until your belly is swollen with my children, then yes. You may call it a marriage." His filthy words are spoken as plain as day.

"What if I say no? What if I want to fuck some other big dumb alien?" The words sound whiny even to my own ears.

Drohako narrows his eyes. "You are mine, and I will kill any other male for looking at you...do not test me, human, or there will be consequences." Though he whispers, it's almost scarier than when he was yelling.

Consequences.

Is it fucked up that the word has me clenching my pussy?

"What if I can't behave myself?" I toy with him.

Maybe if he didn't feed into every brutal fantasy I've ever had, this whole mate thing would be a much harder pill to swallow. But my freshly healed pussy throbs at the thought of him taking what he wants from me, of killing another male for just looking at me.

"You will learn discipline, you will obey me, or I'll restrain you." A jolt of pleasure thrums up my spine, and I sit up at attention.

"Then what?" I ask, my hand finding its way down to my already slick lips. The big brute of an alien cocks his head as he watches me slide my fingers over my clit.

"I never gave you permission to come," he says with a glint in his eye.

"Whoops, guess you should tell me how to earn that privilege, shouldn't you?" I dip a finger into myself.

"Stop," he says through gritted teeth. His fists ball up at his sides as he glares at me.

"Does it make you want to punish me? Does your little human mate make you angry, Drohako?" I buck my hips, finding a rhythm.

Drohako, a male of action, doesn't bother with his words any longer. With two of his massive strides, he bridges the distance between us in the blink of an eye.

With a single fluid motion, he tears the loincloth off his waist. Standing over me, the vee of his groin muscles lead into the swell of his cocks, already thick and drooling. He can act mad all he wants, but I know that his body is screaming for mine. Grabbing his cocks at the root, he pushes them against my mouth.

"Open up, human, prove to me you're worthy of a release."

Drohako wants me to suck his cocks? I was under the assumption that most aliens might not understand what a blow job is...but it seems the Volkroth have no misunderstanding on the art of sucking dick.

He grabs my hair, wrapping it around the back of his hand, and pulls my head forward. My lips are barely open as the head of one of his prehensile cocks pushes past my lips. Just one of them is enough to fill my entire mouth, and as he shoves the second pulsing member in, I can't help but gag. Saliva drips from my mouth as he fucks it. Guttural slurping noises fill the cave.

"Touch yourself," he commands.

When I do, I'm even slicker than before, clit throbbing with a pleasure that hovers near pain. He weaves both hands in my hair, and he pushes himself as far into my mouth as he can go, only a little more than halfway down his girthy length.

"Do you want me to fuck you, human?" he gets out between thrusts.

"Yeshfnugpmh," I gargle as he hits the back of my throat again.

"Do you want my seed dripping out of that swollen cunt of yours?" His breathing is getting uneven, and his balls tighten against his body.

I can't even make out the words to say yes, but God yes, I want him to use me. My mouth is stuffed too full. I taste his sweet pre-cum on the back of my tongue, leaking like he's about to bust. He withdraws and pushes me onto my back.

"Are you wet enough for me?" He slides down my body and hovering his square stubbled jaw over my weeping mound.

"So wet for you," I croak, my throat not recovered from the fucking he just administered.

I expect him to crawl back up my body, to notch his cocks into me and to fuck me until I explode. But I grab the furs I lie on as he drags his wide, rough tongue up my slit.

"What are you?" he asks, the heat of his breath that fans over my pussy driving me insane.

"Human," I breathe, squirming under him.

"Be still," he commands, putting a hand on the small of my belly. "No, what are you to me?" He looks up at me with serious eyes.

"Mate?" I say, unsure. He rewards my answer with a slow and firm lick of my clit.

"Say it again." He bites my inner thigh.

I can't help but arch up, needing more of his touch.

"Mate, I'm your mate!" I yelp as his lips close over my clit and he begins a relentless rhythm of suction and thrumming of the sensitive nub with his tongue.

"Fuck, Drohako, I'm going to come," I mewl under his ministrations.

He pushes two of his thick fingers into me, never stopping his aggressive stimulation of my clit. The muscles of my sex clasp around his hand, begging to be fucked harder. The delicious burn of a building orgasm coils in my belly.

"A little further, keep going, don't stop," I beg as he sucks my clit.

"Wait, you're not allowed to come until my cocks are inside you, human," he says as he lifts his head from my mound.

Wait? I can't wait! I'm almost crossing the precipice, at the point of no return.

"Too close, can't wait," I pant, bucking up against his mouth.

When he growls against my pussy in response, it's just what I need to cross over. His mouth leaves me at the very second I do, and his cocks push into me as my pussy flutters. I spiral into pleasure.

Every inch of his cocks that pushes past my trembling core only heightens my pleasure into pure ecstasy. My vision tunnels as he grabs my hips and lifts them off the ground.

Drohako grunts when I go limp in his hands. I'm so overwhelmed with pleasure that I see literal stars. My senses narrow.

The only thing I can see is his sweat-covered

brow, his black hair sticking to his forehead, and the only sound I can process is the beat of his sac as it slaps into my ass with every vicious stroke.

His cocks coil inside of me, and I feel them knotting themselves together, pushing against my cervix.

"My mate, you're my mate, you're my ma—" Drohako jolts, and his cocks shoots his hot seed into my belly. His thick shafts push deeper still, as if he wants to push his cum as far into me as he can. He is so fucking desperate for it to take root.

His knotted dicks swell and lock inside of me. Even though his thrusting has slowed, they still pump. Drohako collapses on top of me, his colossal body pinning me to the ground.

"Drohako." I wince as he crushes me underneath him. "I can't breathe!"

He groans, eyes closed, and flips us both, still locked together, until I'm straddling him flat on his back. My pussy still throbs around him as I let myself be the one to collapse this time. The sweat of our bodies, the mixture of his cum and my slick, leaves us sticky and panting.

"I like not listening," I mutter into his big purple chest.

An enormous hand slaps my ass, and I clench at the sting. The barbarian's eyes roll back, and he moans in response to the motion of my reaction.

My clenching milks his knot, and his release pushes out of my pussy. He brings another hand down with a crack on the other cheek, and I tense and tug at the tie between us again, an unavoidable response to the pain.

"I thought you didn't want me to move when we're knotted together?" I pant, reaching a hand back to rub my stinging ass.

"Not in the spawning pits...but here in the

homecave, I want your cunt to milk me as long as it can," he moans, as his cocks pump even harder.

"As long as I can?"

I arch a brow as I lean back against his knees, reclining to present him with my knotted pussy. He tucks his chin down, still glistening with my juices, to watch the show. I take his hand and put it over my swollen clit.

"Hit me here," I command with a devious smile.

His eyes narrow, but I get no warning before he cracks his hand against my slit.

"Fuck!" I yelp.

The reaction of his hand against my already oversensitive clit sends sparks to my core. I squirm and clench so hard that he grunts and holds me tightly against his cocks, both of his hands on my hips.

Even though he's not thrusting, it almost feels like he is as his knot expands and contracts.

"Again," I tell him, and he obeys.

Each thwack of his big palm brings me closer to a second finish.

"You're my mate," I moan on the smack that pushes me over the edge.

His knot spasms, and I swear it bulges in my belly. It pushes against my G-spot and when I orgasm this second time, I can feel the rush of wetness as he makes my pussy squirt.

As the aftershocks roll through me, I'm completely boneless. I slump against his warm chest and finally rest. It might not be so bad to be someone's mate after all.

____

CHAPTER SIX

____

I really didn't put up much of a fight for the whole "mated to Drohako" thing, and the alien barbarian almost gives me time to reconsider between orgasms... But maybe it's for the best I'm not overthinking this one too much.

Currently, I'm having trouble forming any thoughts as my alien barbarian mate won't stop eating me out.

I grab a set of his horns and pull with all my might to get him to release my super sensitive clit from between his lips.

My hips press into the ground as I do everything I can to escape his attentions.

But Drohako's tongue doesn't stop, and his fingers push his dripping seed back into my pussy as he does.

Even though his knot released what feels like hours ago, he won't let me find any rest.

"So wasteful of my seed, little human," he growls into the apex of my thighs. "Don't you fucking dare let a drop leave your cunt!"

Once he's scooped the spilled cum from my thighs and plugged it back up into me, he puts two knuckles at my entrance like a cork.

"Drohako, I've got to be more cum than water at this point!" I yelp as his tongue laps firm circles all round my swollen clit.

"Don't care, shut up now, human. Be good for once," he mutters before resuming his sucking.

Another orgasm? I can't let that happen again. There has to be a limit to how many orgasms the human body can handle, right? What if this is the one that makes my heart give out?

When I realize that trying to pry him off by the horns isn't working, I shove my hands down as a barrier between my oversensitive flesh and my alien mate's tongue. He growls, letting one of his sharp teeth break the skin of my knuckle before gathering my wrists easily in his massive palm. He pins my hands against my chest and continues to feast ravenously.

"Drohako, st-stop. It's too much," I whine as my nerves fire so aggressively I'm afraid my brain might short circuit.

"Stop? You were so eager to come just a few minutes ago. I'm just giving you what you want. If the pleasure is too much, consider it a consequence of your own actions." Drohako pops his head up and snarls before diving back down.

It's like I'm running a marathon but actively attempting to avoid the finish line. I'm exhausted. The muscles in my core are burning from overuse. My pussy is probably still gaping from his knot, and my entrance stings where his knuckles plug me up.

I can't come again, I don't have it in me.

At least that's what I tell myself as my muscles coil and tighten.

"I—I—I can't," I sob with each agonizing pulse.

"Be a good fucking girl," he growls, pushing my thigh down as it attempts to snap closed over his head. "Be a good girl and I'll reward you. Listen to your mate."

He speaks as if I could stop the freight train of an orgasm that crashes into me.

Instead of the usual enjoyable clenching feeling, my body shakes uncontrollably.

My eyes roll back as he presses his tongue against me, undulating as some kind of agonizing pleasure rips over my body.

The noises coming from my mouth sound like an injured animal and I'm not sure if I've squirted or wet myself.

Do I even care? It seems like an unimportant detail. I've already lost control of my motor skills.

I can't even remember my own name as Drohako slows his pace. The furious licking of before is replaced by him running his tongue over my outer lips, just skirting the sensitive and swollen flesh of my privates.

Are my eyes shut or open? The only thing in my field of vision is blackness.

I'm still twitching when he gathers me up in his arms. He lays me on some soft platform, and I can hear the sloshing of water.

Starting at my brow, Drohako swipes a wet cloth down my face. My sight slowly comes back into focus, and I see purple hands wringing out red water into the bowl. Slowly and methodically, he wipes the dirt and sweat from my skin. The hours we've spent fucking on the cave floor have tinged my skin crimson, similar to this planet's red earth.

He wets it again and drags it over my tits and torso. I stiffen as his hands dip, expecting him to wash my still throbbing pussy. He pauses at my reaction.

"Calm down human, my tongue cleaned there enough," he says unusually softly.

"Oh, okay," I croak out a little awkwardly.

The cloth drags down the outside of my hips and to my bare feet. I try to tug my foot back as it tickles when he moves the cloth between my toes.

"Stillness, please," Drohako asks with exasperation more than anger.

"Sorry," I tell him, too spent to brat any further.

When he walks away, I wonder what's next. Will I finally sleep? Will he drag me into the healing spring and try to get me back into fucking shape?

Do I dare ask him for rest?

When he comes back, he has a bowl that looks like it was cut from some kind of dried gourd. He dips his fingers in and scoops out a thick and goopy substance.

I push up onto my elbows, groaning as I do, the occasional shake still wracking my body at random intervals.

"What's that?" I ask suspiciously.

"Rendered kurthari fat, with herbs," he says plainly as he warms it between his palms. I can smell the sweet plants as the oils release with the friction of his hands.

"And what exactly are you planning to do with it?" I arch a brow, unsure of where this is going.

"Your reward, as long as you keep behaving." A hint of a smile cracks his face.

I can't go again...and why the fuck does he think he's going to need lube now if he's found it unnecessary for his enormous cocks before?

"Drohako, I really can't fuck. I'm spent—"

"Lie on your stomach, human." He rolls his eyes with annoyance.

"I'm serious, you'll hurt me if we go much longer." I get a panicky edge to my voice.

As he listens, his face softens.

"I will not fuck you. Calm down. Remember, if you listen to your mate, you will be rewarded." He speaks soft and low. The usual spark of viciousness is gone from his eyes.

"Promise?" I ask, only a little desperate.

"Lie down and be quiet," he whispers, putting his slick hands on my hips and turning me over.

My face buries into a pile of furs, and I realize for the first time that he's placed me into some large, curtained bed.

"You have a bed and we've been fucking on the floor all day?" I bark at him, shocked at the revelation.

"You seem to enjoy being fucked into the dirt."

Well, he's probably not wrong.

When his hands grab the meat of my ass, I tense. I can't help it.

"Drohako, please," I whisper, hoping that whatever he has planned won't break me.

His fingers dig deep into one of my hip joints, like he's searching my muscles for something.

"What are you doing?" I swivel my head to get a better view.

He doesn't answer, but lets his fingers glide over my flesh until he finds a spot of tension. His palm presses and kneads a knot in my glute. The pressure is slightly painful, but in a way where my body will thank him later.

"Are you massaging me?" I ask in disbelief.

"Humans must be quite an advanced species to decipher such mysteries," he scoffs sarcastically before moving to my other hip.

"I just thought that you were going to, I don't know—ugh." I grunt as he gets deeply into a ball of muscle.

"You thought I would rape you?" he says coldly.

"I, I mean..."

"I'd fall upon my blade first," he says as he moves to the small of my back. "It's my job to protect my mate and to ensure you're safe and happy to carry our young. Don't you dare imply I'd ever do that again."

His hands move to my neck, and I groan as he pushes the bones of my shoulder blades aside to press the tips of his fingers deeper into the joint.

"But what—fuckohmygodthatfeelsgood—what if..." I trail off as his fingers release what feels like a lifetime of tension.

"What if what?" he asks, picking up my suddenly much more pliable body and tucking it against his as he sits on the bed. His oily palms cups both of my breasts.

"Hey, you said no sex!"

"How is holding your udders sex?"

"One, please never use that word again, and two...I mean, touching usually leads to sex," I tell him, appalled at his choice in words.

"Don't be stupid." He lifts my heavy breasts, instantly taking the tension off my back. "Breathe, deep breaths."

I almost protest, but the sensation of filling my lungs unencumbered by the weight of my tits is a weirdly amazing feeling.

"In through your nose and out through your mouth," he whispers into my ear, cupping and supporting me in a way I only wish a bra could. I relax back into his chest. "Good girl."

"What if I need you to stop? What if it's actually too much?" I keep breathing, closing my eyes as I focus on the rise and fall of his chest.

"Trust me, I won't hurt you any more than you want me to," he whispers.

"Can we have a safe word?" I ask cautiously.

"I do not know this term. What makes a word safe?"

"It's a word that we don't use in regular conversation. That if one of us says it during our time together, we stop. No questions asked."

He hums a little in your ear, as if he's considering the option.

"If it makes you feel secure, I will do this," he says as he releases my breast. His fingertips move to work the tissue near my armpit, making me wince.

"It would," I grit out through the pain. "You can use it too, if you need to."

Drohako laughs with his entire chest, shaking me in the process. "Very funny, human! What word would you like to choose?"

I think for a moment, and the perfect word flies into my mind.

"Udders. You're not allowed to say it unless something is too painful or too intense. Sound good?" I smile, pleased to have all but eradicated that word from his vocabulary.

"But then what will I call these?" he asks, sliding slick hands over my nipples.

"Breasts, tits, boobs, fun bags, literally anything else."

"Fine." He seems disappointed. "If you say 'udders' I will stop, no questions asked."

"Thank you." I tilt my head back to meet his golden gaze.

"It's a simple request. Do not make a bigger deal of it than it is, human." He brushes off the gesture and moves his hands to my thighs, sliding more of the sweet-smelling fat down my sore legs.

CHAPTER SEVEN

Drohako and I have gotten into something close to a routine over the past few weeks.

When I wake, he stuffs me full of weird alien food. There must not be a polite way to decline a meal for the Volkroth because anytime I've wrinkled my nose or pushed a bite away, he refuses to accept no for an answer.

He wants me stuffed in more ways than one.

Once I finish eating, Drohako fucks and uses me for hours. I can't even keep track of how many times I've had to use my safe word for overstimulation alone.

The big purple alien barbarian, to his credit, listens even though he makes a sour face at my refusals.

Then, once I'm spent and slick with seed, he carries me into the healing spring, the planet's blood, as he calls it, and rubs the thick water over the bruised and raw parts of me.

There's this dichotomy inside of Drohako. The brute who wants nothing more than to rut me raw, and the mate who needs to make sure I'm alright.

It makes each side of our encounters all that more intense, to know that he's capable of both.

I chew the rough textured meat, turning my head only to catch him staring at me.

"Do I have something on my face?" I joke, wanting to break the tension.

"No," he mumbles.

There's a few tense moments where his eyes stay locked on me, something I can't read behind his eyes.

It's cut short when Grasyi whines at the cave's entrance, wanting to be let back in from his daily hunt.

Despite its terrifying appearance, the big yellow cat has grown on me. I often wake up to him dropping some giant half-dead bird at my feet. The act isn't one I particularly enjoy, but I understand the sentiment.

"Good boy." I wince as I kick the headless turkey-sized thing off my feet.

He sits back on its muscular haunches, and pants. The feline face contorts to something almost like a smile. If a smile could be so...*toothy*.

"A small one today, eh?" Drohako eyes the carcass that is anything but small to me.

Drohako loves the beast for as much as he complains about him. I witnessed some of his deep and guarded gentleness when I watched him tend to the creature's injured paw. With careful extraction, he removed the large thorn that caused him to limp, with little reaction.

When the creature nuzzled Drohako's face, I was in damn near shock to see him smile.

It's not a smirk or a cunning smile, but a smile filled with warmth. A smile of affection.

He walks over to the creature with a sigh and holds the flap to the homecave open. With one firm slap of his muscular rump, he sends him off into the brutal red world that is this planet.

I take another bite of whatever kill that the cat brought back last night.

"He cares for you, you know," he says before sitting next to me.

"I suppose." I'm preoccupied with chewing through the gristly meat. While I have no complaints about the alien dick here, the food leaves much to be desired.

"Think he'd ever let me ride him?" I ask, mouth full, recalling the few times I've seen Drohako ride him to fetch water or supplies.

"The bond between a mount and rider is a spiritual one. I don't think it's possible." He frowns at my request.

"Even though I'm your mate?" I wiggle my fingers in the air as if the word "mate" is magic.

The corner of his mouth ticks up in amusement.

"That, I'm unsure of. The last Volkroth mated pair was long before I was even born," he says, a bit more wistfully than I expect.

"What? What do you mean?" I'm a bit taken aback. I knew this must not happen for everyone in the breeding pits, but not since before Drohako was born?

"I mean, that this," he wags a finger between us, "hasn't happened in a long time. I've never heard of a Volkroth mating a species other than our own."

"Wait, there are female Volkorth? Where are they?" Surely, they aren't cool with the whole paid spawning season.

"The female Volkroth?" he muses. "They died out, we adapted. We're lucky our young gestate outside a womb, otherwise my species would be doomed."

"So you're telling me that every Volkroth female

just...died?" I'm so confused about how that would even be possible.

"Yes, fewer and fewer females were born until there were none left. Then the males whose seed refused to take in other species' lines died too," he says quietly, trying to look unaffected. "The spawning pits are a necessity, to breed females and introduce genetic diversity. It's the only way we could continue the Volkroth way of life."

"And you mated me, some human from a space station that's a glorified hunk of space junk?"

I'm flabbergasted. What would make me so special?

"You're the first human I've ever seen in the pits." His voice deepens as he puts his huge square hand on my thigh. My muscles instantly stiffen, the anticipation of what's coming quickly heating my core to liquid magma.

"I think I knew what you were when I saw you in the dirt, eyes wide and wet," he whispers, leaning closer.

"Knew what?" I ask, almost salivating with anticipation. He has my body trained to crave his touch.

"That you were different, you were a worthy opponent...you were mine," he growls, clasping the column of my throat.

My eyes roll back as he squeezes the sides of my neck. He pulls me forward against the fur hides I sit on. His body swivels over mine and suddenly I'm face down. His thick limbs are caging me in.

There's a flame-lit shadow spreading out on the floor in front of us. Drohako's silhouette is one of pure power. It gives the illusion of some ripped shadow demon dancing with the crackling fire.

"Mine to do with as I please, to fill every hole as I wish."

I hear a squelching noise as he speaks, then something slick and warm being slathered in the cleft of my ass.

"Drohako," I warn, "I've never put something *there* before, let alone something as *big* as you." I'm nervous at the thought of him fucking my ass with his monster cocks.

"You have your safe word," he mutters as he works the tip of his finger past my tight ring.

"Oh, okay," I breathe, adjusting to the new nerve sensations that he's found.

"I don't want to put both my cocks inside your tight hole," he growls, "just one, so I save the other for your sweet cunt."

He acts like it's no big deal. But just one of his cocks is still the most massive thing I've ever had inside of me.

"Fuck, Drohako." I press my hips back, and he slides further inside, the muscles of my ass resisting as he breeches it deeper.

"I want to stuff you full."

He adds a second finger slowly inside my back door. His other hand finds my clit, stroking it with long, firm strokes. The pleasure he creates at the apex of my legs has things feeling more relaxed around back. I breathe deep, willing my body to accept the fingers he's feeding into me.

It feels...*better than I thought it would*. It's an entirely unfamiliar sensation than when he fucks my pussy, but not a bad one. The sensations grow more pleasurable with each passing second.

"I'll stretch this taut bud until it's good and ready for my cock. It'll fit," he says confidently. "You're made for me, you're my mate."

He pumps his hand more roughly. Spreading his fingers wide, he stretches me further before a third finger works past my subconscious resistance.

There's a burn, but I like it.

Drohako raises my ass up and notches one of his shafts at my pussy's entrance.

He is not gentle with this familiar hole, and I don't want him to be. He slams deep, grunting with the effort it takes to keep his other cock from entering the promised land as well.

I claw at the dirt. The combination of his fingers on my clit and inside my ass and his thick manhood buried deep in my pussy is fucking decadent.

He throbs inside me and my channel clenches.

"I will not go slowly. I need to fill you completely," he groans, about as much warning as I'm liable to get from him.

I am unprepared for the feeling of him stuffing my ass. He has me arching my back like a cat at the burning stretch of his cock. A reflexive hiss leaves my lips.

Drohako, savoring the tightness of me around him, stills his hips as he rakes his hands down the skin of my back.

"Made for me," he growls as he withdraws both cocks nearly completely before slamming himself home again, all while furiously working my clit.

As he fills me, the air leaves my chest in one big hiss.

"Drohako," I sob, unable to parse the current of sensation running through me.

Deeply, he dives back in. I can feel the dual friction of both sides of the thin strip of flesh that separates my channels. Having his cock pounding into my ass makes the shaft in my pussy grind against my G-spot. The impact has me curling my toes.

"So tight, so perfect. Choke my cocks," his voice huffs ruthlessly.

I'm being fucked into a gasping silence as my

face is pushed against the ground. My nerves fire at all once, the intensity almost too much.

I'm clenching my ass tightly as the thrum of oblivion approaches. His heavy balls slap against my cheeks as he picks up his pace.

I draw up tightly, and with a final flick of my clit, I come apart into a seizing storm of pleasure.

"Fuck!" Drohako growls, releasing my clit only to grab me by the hips. He lifts me off the ground as he bounces me on his cocks, one hand pressing hard on the small of my belly while he uses the other to grab me by the throat.

"Do it," I choke out, "empty yourself into me."

I sob, his pounding pushing my orgasm further. The edges of my senses fuzz and blur.

The cock in my ass fires first, pumping thick loads into the uncharted territory. The throbbing shaft in my pussy is quick to follow, and the staggered sensation of both dicks exploding inside me is enough to push me over the edge again.

I shake as he places me face down on the ground again. His cocks futilely search for each other. They seek to knot like they do in my pussy, but their division just lets them probe deeper, leaving me a mewling, overstimulated mess.

There's a pop from the suction as his shafts leave me. My ass gapes, and I can feel the slide of of his seed from both of my holes.

"Good girl." He stuffs a thick knuckle at the entrance of my pussy.

I'm a panting mess. Words lost to some snapping pleasure.

"So good for me, so tight and greedy for my cocks," he coos, laying it on thicker than normal.

He's softer when he needs to be. Gentle, even, for a barbarian.

I don't hate it.

He gathers me up, slipping both our bodies into the warm planet's blood. I'm not even sure I need it, despite the new experience today.

Drohako made sure my ass could take him. He took his time. But as the warm waters wash over, I don't mind the comfort they provide.

He cradles my body as I let my eyes close, trying to ride the wave of endorphins as long as possible.

BEEP.

I snap my eyes open. The digital noise is distinctly out of place in this primitive setting.

"What was that?" I ask my mate in a haze.

Drohako's lip twitches, almost as confused as I am, until some sick realization crosses his face. Slamming his fist into the water, he sends thick droplets of the planet's blood spraying in every direction.

"No, it is too soon." His chest heaves with his quick breaths, the purple of his cheeks intensifies as panic about something washes over him.

"I knew this would come, but I thought I'd have more time, time to figure out a plan. I've been too drunk off the bond, I've failed us." He's angry, and I still have no idea what the fuck is going on.

"What is going on?" I say as calmly as I can muster.

He goes still, unable to say anything. I step toward him, putting a hand on his chest, and look up at Drohako's forlorn face. His hand cups my cheek, a finger straying to trace my ear.

"You're pregnant. You'll be retrieved to go to the nesting grounds soon." His eyes shimmer with some unspoken pain.

I raise my hand up, feeling the metal ear cuff lodged in the cartilage of my ear. A safety measure, they said.

I forgot about the tracking device.
BEEP.
It sounds again, shrill and sharp. An orange light flashes from it, casting a sickly glow on the purple face above me. This thing linked to my vitals knows I'm pregnant.

I'm pregnant.
The thought hits me harder than you would think. Why is it shocking that I signed up for a breeding program, fucked an alien for weeks, and got knocked up? My hand drifts to my stomach. An idea is so much less scary than what's actually happening. Something lives inside me now, a part of Drohako.

"Do we go now?" I ask, still dazed.

"They will come for you," he says, his voice cracking.

"I...we knew this time would come," I say, trying to convince myself that this is fine, part of the plan.

But fuck, this plan went out the window the second I became his mate, didn't it?

"They will not take you from me," he growls, gripping me even tighter.

"Drohako." I pry at his hand as his nails bite into my skin. "Calm down. I'll be back." I cup a hand to his cheek.

"You will not. They will ship you to a different spawning pit in the name of genetic diversity." The barbarian's breathing is becoming frantic. "I will kill anyone who dares to take you from me." He drags us from the pool quickly, grabbing one of the many blades stashed through the cave.

"Drohako, it's okay, we'll talk to them." I rush out as he drags me through the cave, collecting as many weapons as he can strap to his body. "We'll just tell them that we're mates, they'll understand."

Finally, once he's covered head to toe with daggers and swords, he sets me down behind him and sits directly in front of me, blocking my view of the entrance.

"Drohako?" My voice is soft and scared.

"They will not take you from me," he says, holding a blade at the ready, concentration fixed on the cave's opening.

—————

CHAPTER EIGHT

—————

His chest heaves as I step toward him, the blade still raised at some unknown foe.

"Drohako, it's okay, I'm still here," I whisper, trying to diffuse this situation.

When the alien barbarian tilts his massive jaw down, his eyes are black with fury.

"I'll go, just for now. I will convince them to let me come back to you." I try to comfort the alien, who refuses to feel anything other than rage.

"They will not let you come back to me," he says through gritted teeth.

"Drohako, they will—*they must*." Grabbing his hand, I press it to my lips, kissing his scarred knuckles. I'm taken aback when he rips his hand from my grip, grunting with disgust.

"Just listen," I beg him, tugging his palm back. "Listen to your *mate*."

He looks at me with a wary expression, as if the word "mate" breaks him. His defensives seem to fall, and Drohako collapses to his knees. It's as if his body cannot bear its weight. The thought of losing me physically crushes him. His face is no longer taut with anger, but his fists are still balled at his sides.

I take a deep breath, ready to talk some sense into him.

"It will be okay, I will go—"

"Udders," he says, cutting me off.

I jolt, surprised at his response.

"Udders? What does our safe word have to do with this?" I ask, thinking he must be confused.

"If anything becomes too intense...or too painful, we use our safe word," he whispers.

Oh.

A fat tear slides over his purple cheek, a shocking burst of emotion for the barbarian. He seems just as uncomfortable at the display as he swipes away the wetness and quickly steels his expression.

Oh no.

"Drohako, I will convince them we belong together, but to do that, I need to go." I say the words, even though it's not what I want to do. The image of the lone tear on his cheek will be permanently burned into my memory.

"We promised this to each other...you say *udders* and I stop. Now when I finally use this word, you choose to betray me like this?" He stares into my soul, knowing that he's right. "I don't want a stranger to raise our child, not when you're my true mate. Don't leave me." He pauses, placing a hand on the small of my belly. "Don't leave *us*."

His plea hangs in the air, and my heart thumps in my chest.

"I want to stay," I whisper, knowing it's the truth. "I want to stay here with *you*."

Drohako's body relaxes as he lets out a sigh of relief.

"But how would we even do that? They're tracking me, aren't they?" I run a finger over the still blinking ear cuff.

"Do you trust me?" he asks, his eyes shining with a calculating glint.

I almost laugh with absurdness of the question. How could the answer be anything but yes? Do I trust the alien in front of me that holds my face in his huge hands?

"With my life," I tell him.

He reaches behind him, grabbing a scrap of leather. Holding it to my lips, he orders me, "Open your mouth and bite down on this."

I do it, and flinch only slightly as he brings the sharp steel tip of the blade to the shell of my ear.

"I will cut only what I have to," he says matter-of-factly. "Then we set out to the wilderness. My hunting partner, Rahldro, will help us. We have a hunting ground with supplies to hold us over until we can establish a new homecave."

I spit out the leather, anxiety suddenly welling in my stomach.

"Your hunting partner? Is he trustworthy?" It seems from my limited view of the fighting in the spawning pits that survival of the fittest is no joke.

"He is..." Drohako's face twists, as if he's searching for the right words to say. "We have no choice."

"Comforting," I say uneasily.

"It is the reality of things."

"Do you think I'm cut out to be a space pioneer?" I ask, scared of what this new life he has planned might be like.

"We're made to be together, *mate*."

The last word hangs in the air. It feels so different from when he says "human."

I nod, trusting him, letting my chest burn with fondness for him—my mate. He hands me back the piece of leather, and I place it obediently back in my mouth.

All those sparkly warm feelings are cut incredibly short as the tip of his knife curves under the ear cuff. He angles it into my skin and starts prying the connection points out.

Even though I bite down on the strap, I can't stop my hand from shooting up reflexively. Drohako quickly pins it against my body.

"Be still. It's almost free." His purple tongue darts out from his lips in a show of concentration.

"Ugh, fuck, Drohako," I yelp, spitting out the strap again. I feel the last bit of resistance give way and the cuff clinks dully against the floor.

He nearly knocks me over when he starts to stomp the shit out of the tracking device.

I stare in awe as he keeps slamming his foot into the device, tiny metal shards flying free as he works. The orange light flashes again once before it's smashed from existence. He keeps going until I'm not even sure there are pieces of the cuff left.

"Drohako," I say to his unhearing ears, before yelling even louder. "Drohako!"

Finally, I grab his biceps, and he turns. The vein in his forehead throbs, and he tries to catch his breath.

"Let's go," I command, "tell me what you need me to do."

He needs me to focus him, to funnel his rage about the situation into action.

I need to ground my mate.

He takes a deep breath, and his whole demeanor changes as he becomes an alien of action. He tosses me a bag.

"Fill this with as much dried meat as it'll hold. I'll ready Grasyi."

CHAPTER NINE

Paying no attention to the stinging sensation in my ear, I hastily gather as much food as the leather bag can accommodate. Once the off-putting extraterrestrial jerky is nearly spilling out the top, I sling it around my body.

My naked body.

"Drohako," I say gently, understanding that my alien barbarian needs a bit of coddling right now.

"Yes?" he asks while strapping what appears to be a sword bigger than my whole body across his back. The amount of steel he's covered himself with gleams like scales in the cave's firelight.

"So, just hear me out—shouldn't I have clothes if we're leaving?" The reality that I've been naked this entire time really hadn't set in. I mean, he hasn't left me much room to breathe between orgasms, let alone be worried about modesty.

Drohako cocks his head, his eyes scanning my body with a keen observation. Retreating to the pile of furs, he digs until he finds what he's looking for. When he comes back, he has two articles in hand.

"Arms up, mate."

As I do, he drapes an oversized poncho over my

shoulders, engulfing me. As soon as my head pops through, he's already offering me a pair of worn and rugged-looking bottoms.

"You wear pants?" I arch an eyebrow, realizing I've never seen him in anything but the nude.

"Only while riding."

He lashes the leather cord around the waistband of the bottoms. They are equally large. Fiddling with the volume of fabric gathered around my waist, Drohako steps away to observe his handiwork.

"I like you better naked." He frowns, pulling on a duplicate pair of breeches as he does. The powerful muscles of his legs fill out the pants until they strain at the seams.

"Rude. I like you any way I can get you." I drool at the thick bulge of his cocks as he laces up the front. I place my hand on his hip.

"As much as I desire to do that, we must prioritize more important tasks. If you behave, I will reward you at the hunting caves." His eyes roll only slightly as he shakes off my touch.

"Yeah, got it. So, clothes, meat, what next?"

"We hope Grasyi won't throw you, and we set up a new homecave in the wilds." He pats the rump of the terrifyingly large space cat, which he has already told me likely won't allow me to ride him, with a smile.

"Hope, it's such a fun word." Sarcasm drips from my lips as I sauntering toward the pair. "You said he likes me, right? I mean, it can't be too hard to convince him if he already likes me, can it?"

With a hunk of the jerky in my hand, I cautiously extend my arm toward the beast, watching as it sniffs the air, intrigued by the scent. When he snatches the meat from my hand, I can't help but jump in surprise. I snatch back my fingers instinctively when I catch sight of his oversized canines, a thrill of fear rushing through me.

"Mere morsels of meat will not inspire the bond between rider and mount...it's deeper than that," he says as he grabs the big cat's reins. "You must earn his trust through tolkha."

My translator chip struggles to keep up with the last word.

"Tolkha?" I ask, concerned once again about what my horny desires have gotten me into.

"Tolkha is a test, a challenge. You will mount Grasyi, and he will attempt to throw you...but he will fail, because you are my mate. You are strong enough to carry on my bloodline." He thumps his chest in some masculine display.

Drohako is much more sure of me than I am of myself. I have no desire to ride a giant bucking tiger.

That sounds like literally the last thing I want to do.

"Is this the best idea? I mean, won't that be bad for the baby?" I put a hand over my fur covered stomach.

"Don't be foolish, mate. My bloodline will be strong enough to handle this," he scoffs at the implication that the fetus I carry is weak.

"If you say so, big boy," I squeak out nervously.

"Follow me." He leads me through the cave's entrance. "We'll be at our new home in the wilds before the moons rise."

I follow, and my eyes struggle to adjust. Although the cave's fires kept me out of the dark, I haven't left the rocky home since my arrival. The blazing sun and humidity of the Volkroth planet blast me in the face as I go outside for the first time in weeks.

I raise my palm to shield my eyes. Drohako stands, Grasyi's halter in one hand, waiting for me.

When I finally catch up to them, my barbarian grips me under the armpits, lifting me up.

"Grip him tighter than your cunt grips my cocks," he whispers as my head passes his own.

"Not the time for sexy thoughts, my ass," I mutter, more than a little terrified, as I spread my legs and grab the reins from his purple hands. While keeping the strip of leather in my grip, I wrap my arms around the beast's neck. My thighs and toes dig into his sides.

"So what happens if he throws me off? Do we have to walk?"

"He will be given the chance to eat you if he so chooses. Hold strong mate! Your reward will be a pleasurable one," he says almost sweetly before taking his hands off Grasyi's yellow fur and jumping back.

EAT ME?

As soon as his hands leave the beast, the cat's muscles tense. It's as if everything was fine until he realized it was me mounted on his back.

A low hiss builds in his throat, and he crouches, his front legs low, shifting his weight to the front. I slide, but only slightly, my grip strong and true. The cat turns his long neck and stares me directly in the eyes, his slitted pupils narrowing. My head is tucked against his shoulder blade, and my arms are wrapped tightly around his neck. My face is mere inches away from his snarling and drooling mouth when he turns to look at me.

I slam my eyes shut as he huffs loudly. His breath, akin to the trash mouth of a house cat, is hot and disgusting. I switch to breathing out of my mouth to avoid the smell. When his threatening growl doesn't unseat me from his back, he bucks.

Once at first, but the motion repeats more quickly and violently as he speeds up his motions.

He spins in a tight circle—angry snarls and hisses escaping his wet mouth.

My arms and legs ache with effort, and I really wish he would change directions. He whips his body in concentric circles, roiling my stomach.

"Hold tight!" Drohako's voice settles into the edges of my hearing, through the whirling noise of wind.

The motion goes on forever. I'm sick to my stomach and don't know how much more I can endure.

"Fucking Grasyi, you like me—remember?" I yell, thinking maybe I can soothe the savage beast with just a reminder alone.

Adjusting my hold on the animal, my hand almost slips. I reach up to his fluffy ear and grab the bit of fur just underneath it, digging my nails in tightly against his skin.

Grasyi stops his spinning abruptly, his neck twitching at my new hold. He leans his head toward my hand.

"What's he doing?" I yelp, unsure if this is some part of the tolkha, but I'm just happy the spinning has stopped.

"I...I don't know," Drohako says.

In this momentary stillness, I move my fingers against Grasyi's neck once more. Letting my nails slide down the muscles of his throat, I scratch the giant cat's neck.

I'm shocked as Grasyi purrs.

"Is he trying to nuzzle me?" I ask incredulously. The cat's vibration tickles my skin.

"Grasyi is indeed being affectionate with you... but that's not how tolkha is supposed to go. You're supposed to have your will win over his." Drohako seems confused but impressed.

"There's more than one way to skin a cat—if petting this big, stinky kitty makes it stop spinning, I'll keep doing it," I say through gritted teeth, willing my nausea to pass.

"Technically, it's working." Drohako almost seems disappointed that I've cuddled my way out of what is supposed to be some ultimate test.

"Yeah, great, can you, um, get me down from here?" I ask, the world still spinning.

Drohako rushes to my side and lifts me gingerly from the cat, setting me right on my own two feet.

"I'll set up our supplies bags, and you...you can wait for me to finish." He sets to work and starts talking about the wilds and the location of the hunting cave, but I can't hear him.

I'm still lost in some motion sickness haze.

"...do you agree?" His voice booms back into focus.

"Sure," I mutter before the watering in my mouth is too intense to fight any longer.

I lean over and spill my dried meat lunch on the dusty red sands of the planet. When I stand back up, Drohako winces.

"Are you going to do that again, or can we be on our way, human?"

"Wow, love the concern for my wellbeing," I say sarcastically.

He huffs through his nostrils, and a look of disgust passes over him.

"I only ask because..." He pauses, unsure if he wants to admit something.

"Spit it out." I gesture a circling motion with my hands.

"Because I am"—he scowls as the next word leaves his lips—"sensitive to the odor. I would prefer to keep my food inside my stomach on our journey."

"You have a sensitive stomach?" I laugh, the thought a wild one.

"It is not funny," he pouts.

"I mean, it's a little funny. You, a big bad barbarian Volkroth, can't handle the smell of puke?"

Despite the great and dramatic escape we have planned, I can't stop giggling at the thought of Drohako having a delicate constitution.

Before I'm able to stop laughing, his gigantic hands set me roughly onto Grasyi, and he mounts behind me.

I look up and see his scowl. "It's okay to have, like, one weakness, you know." I try to comfort the brooding alien through my stifled chuckling.

"It is not. The Volkroth kill the weak," he says solemnly.

"I'm weaker than you. Do I have no place with your people, then?" I pose the question to him, realizing that if I'm staying here for good, it might need to be addressed.

"As my mate, you are my people. My son, in your belly, is our people." Drohako wraps an arm around me, settling his hand over my womb.

"A son?" How does he know what the gender of our baby is?

"Without a Volkroth female, only males are born. He is strong because you are strong. If you were weak, you could not accept my seed. We are together. Nothing else matters."

CHAPTER TEN

At some point in the journey, I fell asleep against Drohako's back. There's something soothing about Grasyi's feet padding on the dusty ground.

My eyes flutter open, only to be met with a landscape that falls far short of the wild, untamed beauty I was expecting.

"Drohako," I whisper as he guides the cat to round the corner of a very austere looking building. "Where are we?"

In the dim light of the night, my eyes wander, taking in our surroundings. The towering structure in front of us casts a shadow that obscures the moon's gentle glow.

"Quiet, we're at the nesting grounds." He slips a hand quickly over my mouth as I gasp.

The nesting grounds? Isn't this the one fucking spot he doesn't want to be?

"We need a nesting pod. Our child won't survive for long without one," he tells me, all while keeping his hand clamped tightly over my lips. "I should have secured one earlier, but your cunt has obviously drained all the blood from my brain."

Frustrated, I sink my teeth into his rough, calloused fingers with all my might.

Drohako, unaffected by my efforts, rolls his eyes, but releases his hand all the same.

"Why didn't you tell me we were coming here?" I whisper, annoyed.

"Because I can handle this. It's a quick stop, we'll be gone before long." He says with some macho posturing that pisses me off.

"We're a team asshole," I mutter. "You tell me the plan, always."

I keep my scowl even as he dismounts the big cat and lifts me off his back like a doll.

"Fine," the brute agrees.

"So let's go in there and get the damn pod and then get the hell out of Dodge, yeah?"

I tighten the knot on my pants, cursing the fact that my attire is far from practical. What I wouldn't give for some fucking leggings right about now.

"Informing you of the plan is a much different request than including you in it." His lip curls back in disbelief, as though he can't fathom that I'm re-questing to accompany him.

"So you're just going to leave me out here? That doesn't seem any safer!"

As I cross my arms and pout, he reaches for a dagger on his hip, carefully transferring it into my hands.

"I don't even know how to use a knife," I complain.

A look of surprise crosses his face as his eyebrows shoot up.

"Put the blade into any soft spot you can reach. Don't talk your way out of a confrontation, I know that mouth of yours. You go for your opponent's eyes, groin, throat. Inflict as much damage as you can and when we're safe at the hunting cave, I'll teach you the proper way to wield a blade." He seems overly confident in my skills. "And Grasyi will rip the throat out of an attacker well before you even realize their presence."

I feel the presence of the enormous feline behind me, its claws tugging at the fabric of my pant leg, dragging me toward the ground. Once I'm seated, he wraps his body around me, resting his enormous head on my lap.

"I don't like this." I scowl up at Drohako. "Hurry, be safe, don't do anything stupid."

"You worry about me for nothing. I am the strongest in my clan," he says as he saunters toward a door at the far side of the wall. With a forceful swing of his sturdy leg, he kicks the door so hard that it almost breaks off its hinges.

"Don't be a dick, don't show-off—you have to come back to me, to *us*," I whisper, placing a gentle hand on my stomach.

The heaviness of my words lingers in the air. Deep within me, a tiny life is growing. In this moment, I need Drohako to understand the gravity of his actions, to realize that his choices not only affect him but the future within me.

In a momentary lapse, Drohako's haughty demeanor falters, and a flicker of fear crosses his face.

Just as quickly as it faltered, the mask slides back up.

"You have my word. Now stay put." He jabs his pointer finger in the air at me.

I listen for once. Staying put, I trace the stripes on Grasyi's head with my fingernails as he purrs. I count his whiskers and once I've done that three times in a row, it doesn't do much do calm my anxiety. I lift his hulking head as the cat grumbles and shift the direction my legs are going. The adjustment just leaves my thigh full of pins and needles, and I try to flex my foot to get the blood pumping again.

Annoyed by my incessant squirming, Grasyi places a heavy paw on my leg, demanding stillness.

"You're a moose." I shove his leg to the side.

Petting his yellow fur, I continue to wait, my eyes locked on the open door.

But with all this waiting comes thoughts, and bad ones. This plan doesn't seem well thought-out. It seems really risky. Why wouldn't we wait to do this?

A ball forms in the pit of my stomach.

What if Drohako doesn't come back?

I have little time to spiral into my own thoughts as a bright flash and heat pours out of the door.

My breath catches in my throat as a charred Drohako comes flying through the doorway, arms wrapped tightly around some kind of plastic pod.

His body hits the ground with a crack, and I can actually hear the wind knocked from his chest.

Grasyi scrambles to stand, his claw pushing deeply into my skin. The rush of adrenaline as I hurry to Drohako's side masks the pain, making it feel dull and distant.

As I roll him onto his side, his eyes remain closed, giving no hint of his consciousness.

"Drohako!" I thwack him hard on the back.

His eyes shoot open as he's gasping for breath. When his gaze locka with mine, he coughs and sweeps me into his arms. As he gets his legs underneath him, he wobbles unsteadily. But with each bounding leap, his confidence surges.

"What the fuck happened?" I yelp as he throws me over Grasyi's back, stuffing the egg-shaped device into the rucksack on the cat's hips.

He swings his own leg over, mounting the beast.

With a kick to its ribs, we're off like a shot. The surrounding darkness grows as we ride into the night.

As we gallop into the darkness, I can hear the raised voices and the clank of boots. They're after us, but compared to the feline, they're too slow to catch us.

"Complications." Drohako kicks again, and Grasyi pushes us even faster into the night.

"Complications caused a fucking explosion?" I demand an answer from him, turning my body as much as I can to get a better look at him as we ride.

Noticing my struggle, he quickly intervenes and flips me around. Now, facing him, my legs intertwine with his as I straddle both the cat and the alien.

"I have the nesting pod. It shouldn't matter how it was obtained," he grunts out.

I'm ready to yell at him again, to give him a piece of my mind, but as I brace my hand against his side, I feel wetness. When I pull my hand back, it's covered with his black blood.

"You're hurt!" I squeak, quickly putting my hand back to apply pressure to his wound.

"It is nothing." He blinks rapidly as the dust from the cat's paws flies into the air.

I jab a finger close to the wound. I shouldn't—it's cruel. His body recoils at my touch.

"Nothing?" I parrot back to him. "You get us to that cave as fast as you can!" I tell him before wrapping my other arm around his torso and burying my face against his wooly chest.

"I thought you didn't know how to stab," he winces as I reapply pressure.

"Shut up," I say as tear fall from my eyes.

I'm angry, so why the fuck am I crying?

What started as a casual arrangement for rough sex has grown into a connection that goes beyond physical intimacy. I haven't wanted to admit it before, but the constant knot in my stomach and the racing thoughts are forcing me to confront the undeniable fear of losing him.

You know what this emotion is.

"I love you, idiot."

"You're a warrior, whether you admit it or not," he says, putting his free arm around my waist.

CHAPTER ELEVEN

A jungle spreads out before us, so different from the dusty red steppes I've seen on the rest of this planet. Like a mirage or an oasis, it is teeming with life.

Alien animals swing from the heavy vines that drape over the full golden foliage. The trunks of the trees twist in ways that seem too delicate to support their massive canopies. There must be some magic behind their design.

Lost in the enchantment of this new world, I barely register the feeling of Grasyi stumbling over his own feet.

It feels like time slows down as I'm forcefully thrust forward, unaffected by whatever is holding the big cat's movement at bay. The inertia speeds up my inevitable face-plant into the powdery dirt.

I shut my eyes tight, waiting for impact.

There's a tugging at my belly, and a twisting motion that has my body spinning. I feel Drohako's warm chest at my back. His arms circle my stomach protectively, and although the collision with the ground is abrupt, my alien mate absorbs most of the impact.

It takes a moment before I can breathe properly, the wind knocked out of my chest.

Once I regain some of my composure, I realize that Drohako's arms are limp around me. I twist around, cupping the side of his cheek.

As I pull his face toward mine, blood wells from a forehead cut at the edge of his hairline. The rock underneath his head is small, but jagged.

Drohako is knocked out cold.

I panic, cursing this stupid planet for not having helmets, and put my palms agains the cut. Alien blood has to clot and slow with pressure like humans, right? I examine his earlier wound, wrapped in a makeshift bandage. No further bleeding there, so I must be right.

As the fear of something more sinister than a temporary blackout gnaws at me, I rack my brain, attempting to piece together what transpired.

I scan the treeline, not seeing a single trace of Grasyi... but when I hear him snarl directly above me, I lift my eyes higher, realizing that the giant cat is caught in some primitive snare.

Despite his best efforts, he can't lift its heavy body high enough to bite through the rope that's suspending his four paws above him.

"Did you think you'd get away from the Volkroth, human? That there wouldn't be safeguards against this kind of thing?" A deep voice booms from the thicket of golden leaves.

His boots crunch heavily on the underbrush as he steps into the light.

A Volkroth, smaller than Drohako but nonetheless intimidating, comes closer to me. The larger horn on the left side of his head is cut short, extra noticeable with his cropped hair. He brings his forefinger and thumb up to his chin, appraising me with a devious smile.

"All this trouble for a little thing like you? Seems such a waste." He keeps advancing toward me, and I shake my unconscious protector.

Please wake up, please Drohako...

"I was shocked that Drohako would bring such dishonor to the Volkroth, trying to steal away a bit of human cunt for himself. He's done his job, bred you well, and now we all reap the benefits of continuing our species. He can't just take you...your baby belongs to all of us."

My voice sticks in my throat as the terror finally sets in.

"My hunting partner, my confidant, a true disgrace," he looks at Drohako's body with such disgust that I'm finally able to find my voice.

"We're mates, he told me. I swear he's just trying to keep me safe!" I plead with Rahldro, unsure of what he plans to do with me.

His steps falter when he hears me say the word "mate."

"Mate? Not possible—you lie!" he spits, finally close enough to grab my wrist.

As he rips me from Drohako's still unmoving body, he's full of rage. Somehow, my plea to honor the matehood has had the opposite effect I intended.

"You're hurting me... Drohako won't stand for this!" I yelp, attempting to wrench my wrist from his grip.

"He won't care much about anything anymore." The brute laughs as he throws me over his shoulder. "In fact, maybe I'll claim you as my own in the spawning pits once you're back from the nesting grounds—I've never had something so fragile as a human before."

The Volkroth keeps running his mouth about what he'd like to do to me as I dissociate. My mind slips back to when Drohako first held me like this. How he slung me over his shoulder at our initial meeting. The fear then only heightened my excitement.

Now, as I'm dragged from my motionless mate, it only fills me with dread.

"We can't just leave him here!" I kick my feet against the stranger. "He's your friend!"

"Friend? He's an enemy of state. His brain must be addled beyond help if he's telling you that your his mate. That is not possible!" He's so angry, and I don't know if it's at me, or that I represent something he thinks he'll never have...a mate.

"Please, we can't let him die here." I'm begging, done trying to reason with him.

"Don't worry, the jirion hounds will take care of him."

No, that's not possible.

I run my hands over his chest, fingers searching with unhinged desperation.

"Your 'mate's' body isn't even yet cold, human, and here you are, ready to be rutted again?" The Volkroth laughs with his entire chest, so convinced of the fact that I'd easily give up my mate.

His laugh is cut short as I finally grab one of the many blades that the Volkroth like to keep strapped to their bodies. With every bit of my strength, I forcefully drive the sharp point of the blade into the vulnerable flesh of his neck.

He gurgles as I twist the dagger, fiery blood running down my hand, the liquid sputtering from between his dark purple lips. When he falls to his knees, I regain my footing, kicking off of him as he face-plants into the ground. The bastard clutches at his neck, his body slowly draining of its natural color, mewling around on the ground like the worm he is.

"I tried to tell you," I growl, "we're mated. He is mine and I am his. It's us against the world." He turns his head, his eyes wide with shock. "You should have listened."

He tries to speak, but he can't make the correct noises with his injury. I swear his lips form the word 'mate'.

His movements slow as his skin turns gray.

It didn't have to be like this.

Only when I hear Drohako cough his way back to the realm of the living does my rage subside.

I rush to his side as he struggles to sit up.

"What happened?" he croaks, his voice so hoarse it's almost a whisper. When he touches my hand, his brows draw together. He pulls his fingers back from mine, and they're slick with blood.

The panic spreads over his face as he wipes my cheek frantically with his hands. "Are you hurt?"

"No, it's okay now. Do you think you can stand?" I ask as he continues to clean my skin.

His eyes are wild. "The blood! Where did the blood come from?"

"Don't worry, it's not mine. The blood is yours and the sad excuse for a Volkroth over there."

He follows my outstretched thumb to the dead alien behind us.

"Rahldro? Did he hurt you?" He's not any calmer when he unsteadily clambers to his feet.

I rush to his side, wrapping an arm around his hips, as if he would show weakness by leaning against me.

He doesn't, of course, but instead hurries to the dead Volkroth, now lying face down in a pool of his own quickly coagulating blood, and stomps on his skull with brutal force.

The sickening sound of bones cracking echoes through the air as they collide with the blood-soaked mud. Despite having just slit the dead alien's throat, I quickly avert my gaze from the macabre sight.

Only when Drohako wraps me up in his arms, tucking my chin against his chest, do I refocus my attention.

"Did he hurt you, mate?" he asks softly.

"No, quite the opposite," I whisper. "He was too weak to continue his bloodline. It dies with him."

Pride sparks behind Drohako's eyes, and he cups my blood-soaked face in his hands. He crashes his mouth against mine with a hungry, desperate kiss.

"You are perfect," he mutters against my ear as he breaks away.

Drohako groans as I squeeze the coil of his members through his pants. They pulse, hardening at my touch. We both almost just died, but there's something about victory that makes me slick with want. Maybe I'm becoming a true Volkroth mate after all.

"I will have you stuffed full of my cocks before long, but for now, we ride."

He swiftly grabs a curved blade and hurls it toward a nearby tree trunk, the sound of metal meeting wood echoing through the air. Grasyi is taken by surprise as the blade severs the fibers of the snare rope, causing him to crash heavily onto the ground with a loud thump.

The cat coughs, shaking his head a few times before stalking over to the ruined body of my attacker. He rips a juicy bit of flesh from the dead Volkroth's haunch and swallows it whole. Grasyi wrinkles his nose before gripping the torso in his giant maw, flinging the body off the path and into the thick underbrush of the forest.

With a satisfied snort, he looks back at us as if we're the ones lollygagging.

"To the hunting cave."

Drohako grabs me by the waist, and we mount the feline quickly. Drohako settles me over his legs and facing his chest, his free hand pulling me against him protectively. With a snap of the animal's reigns, we're sprung into motion.

The wind whips against my back, and it's cold as the blood dries. We don't speak as we gallop to our new home. It gives me time to process what just happened.

"I don't want to do this without you," I whisper into his sternum. "I know I said it before, but I love you—I mean it."

I can sense his breath coming to a halt, if only for a moment. His hand glides up my spine, and I can feel the warmth of his touch as he cups the back of my head. Tilting it back, my mate leans in and kisses me.

Instead of the usual fevered, crushing kisses, he surprises me with something tender and yielding, like a whisper against my skin. I open my mouth to him, eager to accept whatever he will offer, completely surrendering myself.

Though I expect him to stop our ride, to take me here in the forest, he doesn't. Drohako notches his head over mine, eyes forward on the trail ahead, when his hand travels back down and slips between us.

Without words, his thick and calloused fingers find my clit.

"Drohako." My breath comes in pants as he runs circles around the bundle of nerves until my pussy weeps with slick.

"You are a good mate," he whispers into the

wind as we ride. It's a simple statement, but there's a strained emotion behind it.

Instinctively, I reach for his hardening cocks that press against my labia through his thin loincloth. I can feel his pulsing need, and I want nothing more than to sate it.

We're safe, and I want to show him how much I want him.

"No."

He pushes my hand aside and keeps circling my throbbing clit.

"I just want—"

"Be quiet. What you want is of no importance. I want you to come."

I feel him slide inside me, his fingers expertly caressing my g-spot while his thumb teases my aching nub.

I'll give him what he wants.

"You are a warrior," he breathes over my head. "A warrior who deserves this pleasure."

I buck as Graysi comes down hard on the ground in tandem with his thrusting hand. It hurts just in the way I need.

"I'm yours," I whine, reaching my arms up behind his neck, needing something to ground me.

"Mine."

His pace becomes more frantic, and he pushes a third digit inside of me, pushing my channel wide.

"You will come when all my fingers are inside you," he commands. "I will feel your tight and grasping cunt around my hand...Is that clear?"

"Fuck, yes. Please stuff me full!" I'm riding his hand, my honey dripping down to his wrist. He pushes deeper, his thumb flexing back to its max angle. His hand is so large that his pinky easily touches the ring of nerves around my asshole.

The pad of his thumb rubs my clit from side to

side. The deep pressure of his actions makes my pussy clench erratically over him. I won't last long like this.

"I'm going to come," I mewl against him, my ass cheeks squeezing and my legs going straight as my body searches for release.

"Not yet," he barks, and he slides out and repositions his hand. "Tell me you want it. You want me to fuck you with my entire hand."

"I want you, I want anything you'll give me."

With all his fingers and thumb pinched together, they push inside me. I'm so wet, but his hand is huge. I worry it won't fit, that I'll fail him.

But my mate knows what I can handle. He pushes past the ring of resistance and slides up the second set of knuckles. The motion of Grasyi's running has the broadside of his hand sliding up and down my clit.

"I can't stop it," I pant. "Go further, I want you all the way in before I co—"

Before I can finish my begging, he slams his hand home. It burns as the widest part slips inside me, but as soon as I clamp down on his wrist and he spreads his fingers inside me, I explode.

My pussy pulses like it's trying to eject his hand, and a torrent of wetness floods out of me. As he fucks me through my orgasm, my whole body shakes and I'm unable to cope with the sensations.

"You're a good mate," he repeats as he slides out of me and grips me before I can slip off the beast below us.

CHAPTER TWELVE

The entrance to the hunting cave is nearly invisible. Golden vines twine over the leather door flap, nearly obscuring it from view.

Sweat drips off my brow. The humidity of the jungle is so different from the dusty deserts of this planet. I find it hard to believe these two ecosystems exist so close to each other.

Drohako removes the saddle bags from Grasyi and sets them near the rocky wall of the cave.

Pushing through the saffron-colored brush, I notice the sweat on my arms mingling with the blood of the fallen alien attacker.

I took someone's life, extinguishing it in a single act. A full-fucking-grown Volkroth warrior.

And he fucking deserved it.

I think about my life before, how I wouldn't be able to do what I had just done. But things are different now. I love an alien barbarian, I'm carrying his child, and we've run away from what little civilization exists on this planet.

I should feel worse about murdering someone, shouldn't I?

Drohako's hand caresses along the messy skin of my arm.

"Your first kill?" he asks, although I can tell that he already knows the answer when I nod. "You are strong, you protected our family—wear his blood with honor."

Our family.

I push my way through the overgrowth on the door and into the cave.

As the leather flap snaps free from the grasping vines, dirt sprays and I cough, my lungs assaulted by the dust.

The hunting cave is even more primitive than I expected. Unlike where we've fled from, there are no comforts. No furs line the sleeping space, the fire pit is tiny, and a thick layer of dust coats everything.

"You don't get to do much hunting, do you?" I ask with a sarcastic smile.

"Hunting seasons are short, especially in spawning years." He shrugs, pushing past me.

Drohako removes the incubation pod from his satchel as if it was the most fragile thing in the world. His thick fingers struggle to hold the tech just barely bigger than a gallon of milk.

"Hard to think you were ever that small." I sigh as I flop down and pat my slightly swollen belly. "I feel like I can't even feel him in there, you know?"

A panicked look flashes across his purple face.

"I mean, he's in there, but I thought it would feel different—like a parasite."

My alien frowns, and I get that my choice of words has me sounding less than enthused.

"What I mean is, it doesn't feel wrong—it feels natural, like it was meant to be."

When I look back up at my mate's face, his gaze softens.

"It's fate," he tells me. "Come, the pod needs a blood sample to activate."

He reaches his scarred hand out to me, pulling me to standing. When he taps a button along the incubation pod's side, a robotic arm pops out.

"It's strange Volkroth's births are so high tech, isn't it? Because, well..." I gesture broadly to our surroundings. The primitive cave isn't really where I would expect the Volkroth to live after seeing this little space-age orb of white metal and glass.

"We choose to live in the ways of our ancestors —but we've adapted to breed without female Volkroth, and it's mostly thanks to this tech." He keeps talking even after the little robot arm pokes my finger with a quickly appearing needle.

"Ouch!" I yelp as Drohako grabs my hand to prevent it from recoiling from the machine.

"Still, it'll be over in a second," he mutters as he watches the collection tube meet the small droplet of blood welling on my fingertip. With a whoosh, the machine sucks the sanguine fluid away.

As the blood enters the pod, it glows with an orange light. The intensity pulses like a heartbeat.

"Done. That wasn't so bad, now was it, my tiny warrior?" His face is filled with pride as he stares down at my blood-covered body.

"Well, no, but—"

He interrupts my words by sucking my finger into his mouth, his rough tongue licking the needle's wound.

"I promised you pleasure earlier," he growls as my finger drops from his lips. The sound of his voice is making my pussy quickly slicker, as if on his command.

When his hand drifts lower, skirting the hem of my wrap, I grab his wrist.

"Stop."

Maybe I'm still full of adrenaline from the attack, or maybe this feeling has always been under the surface—but I want to be in control for the first time in my life.

"Mate?" His body is frozen, maybe shocked by my command.

"I think I'd like to call the shots this time," I whisper to my barbarian.

"That's new." Drohako cocks an eyebrow. The muscles of his body relax slightly, but his eyes bore into me with a new intensity. "So, what do you want?"

"I want you to listen, but don't worry—you'll enjoy yourself if you do. Will you be a good boy for me?"

His pupils dilate, and he looks like he can taste colors as he gazes at me with hooded eyes.

"If that's what my mates wants, a *good boy* is what she'll get."

"I need something comfortable to lie down on," I say with an unpracticed coolness that surprises us both.

Drohako swiftly steps past me, pushing the leather flap out of his way. He grabs the saddlebags from outside. Once back indoors, he kicks some dead leaves and twigs away, clearing a spot on the dirt floor.

He looks at me with a pleased smile as he unrolls a few of the thick yellow furs from our former home.

"This will do." I shrug off my makeshift clothing, already feeling one hundred percent better than before. There's something so natural about wearing nothing at all around Drohako, and that makes my heart sing.

His gaze on my naked body is that of a predator's, hungry and all-consuming. I lie down slowly, deliberately, spreading my legs so he can take in the view.

He inhales sharply and pushes the heel of his hand down over his loincloth, onto his quickly hardening bulge.

"Who said you could touch yourself?" I drawl as my finger traces up my slick lips. "I don't think I gave you permission."

"I thought this was supposed to be fun." He scowls, clenching his fists at his sides. I don't let the fact that he's still listening to me go unnoticed.

"It will be, because the anticipation is part of the pleasure."

Whatever's possessed me to be so bold, I love it. Could it be that letting myself be used like I've always wanted has me finding some new confidence? Have I found my power through being submissive?

I rub small circles over my clit. Drohako's breath catches as he watches me work.

"I want you to want me, to feel every pang of desire."

I twist my nipple with my free hand, not even attempting to stifle the moan that falls from my lips.

"Can I touch you if I can't touch myself?" His voice is needier than I've ever heard it before.

"Are you uncomfortable? Does my having the control cause you this agony?" I ask, dipping my fingers into my opening and thrusting deep. "Don't you wish it was your cocks plunging inside me?"

"Is torture your idea of fun? Does the Volkroth babe inside of you harden your heart like a barbarian?" Despite his suffering, he smiles. His eyes hold a menacing glint.

"Seeing you squirm is fucking delicious, a reward all in itself." I pick up my pace, and throbbing need ebbs through my core. "Ask me for what you want."

Drohako licks his lips, stepping closer.

"I want to taste you," he growls.

"Then crawl and beg me for the honor. Prove to me you want it."

Drohako, the mighty alien warrior that he is, drops to his knees with a thud. He rakes his nails over the dirt floor, pushing his glorious ass high. Each scrape of his fingers over the ground sends shivers up my spine.

When he finally reaches me, he presses his lips against my trembling skin, worshipping every inch of me with fervent kisses. I moan in ecstasy as he continues to worship at the altar of my pleasure. His tongue laps up my honey, teetering me on the edge of bliss.

We're both consumed by our primal desires, oblivious to the world around us, fueled by an insatiable hunger for each other's bodies.

"Make me come, mate," I hiss as I buck my hips, threading my fingers through his coarse hair and wrapping them around his horns.

Drohako probes his fingers into me, spreading me wide with his hands alone. When he sucks on my clit, my core pulses sharply and I shatter.

My legs attempt the snap shut over his ears, but he pushes them open. His tongue is unrelenting.

"Stop!" My voice is hoarse as I yell.

Despite his history of loving my overstimulation, he does. With just one word from me, he immediately ceases his ministrations. He's under my command, after all.

"You've done such a good job, you deserve a reward—"

"Serving you, mate, is enough." He pulls himself

up until his strong jaw rests on my stomach. His face glistens with my juices.

He brings his hand to either side of my hips, kissing the small swell on my stomach. He stares adoringly at the pooch and the promise that lies within.

CHAPTER THIRTEEN

Beep. The sound cuts through the fog of sleep.

Beep. I shift, but the weight of Drohako's body keeps me pinned to the dirt floor of the cave. My hulking mate actually fell asleep in the space between my legs, long after I had passed out from his attentions.

Beep. The noise is accompanied by a soft orange glow, the light flooding over Drohako's purple face as it flashes.

"Hey," I rasp as I reach down and shake the slumbering giant's shoulder.

He blinks rapidly as I rouse him, bringing up a hand to scrub over his face and beard. When he looks up at my face, he gives me a sleepy smile.

Beep.

That smile drops as soon as he registers the sound. The amber light only highlights the shadows of his drawn brow, his face becoming deadly serious.

He scrambles to sitting, leaving me worried.

"Drohako, what's going on?" I spin around to face whatever danger now presents itself. I did just kill a man in self-defense, after all. Surely, I'm ready for anything.

Behind me, the incubation pod flashes and sounds, its high-tech facade so out of place in the primitive hunting cave.

"It's time," my mate grunts.

I thought I was ready for anything... *but childbirth?*

"So, what do we do? Are you sure it's big enough... Wait, how do we get him out?"

The blood drains from my face...how did I not think this far ahead? The realities of the fact that I need to get whatever is in my womb out and into the shiny metal pod are finally hitting me.

"Well, we have the pod..." he nods, wringing his hands together.

I wait for him to finish the sentence, to give me the important details on Volkroth childbirth.

"Drahako..." My voice comes out higher than I expect.

He turns his gaze to me with wide eyes. Something like fear crosses them, which is a strange emotion for me to see play across his face. It seems something far too fragile for him.

"I don't know," he finally admits.

The words leave my stomach in my throat as my anxiety ramps.

"So neither of us knows what to do?" I squeak, subconsciously holding the tiny swell of my belly.

"I can figure this out," he says with some renewed confidence as he approaches the pod.

"That would be amazing, because I don't know what's going on here." A nervous little laugh escapes my lips.

Lifting the white orb from its stone perch, he flips it over as if checking for some hidden access point.

"So, have you ever seen one of these in action?"

I mutter as it dawns on me that technology isn't my mate's strong suit.

He looks at me incredulously.

"I am not some gelded nursery attendant," he scoffs, offended.

"*Gelded?* You know what? We'll double back to that later. I assumed that if you stole the pod, you at least know how it works." I sigh with exasperation.

He frowns and offers me the blinking mystery.

"I needed to make sure no one would take you from me... Your safety eclipsed all my other worries... Including this."

Our matehood has him flustered in ways that aren't very helpful, but it makes my heart ache all the same. I want to soothe the harshness of my last comment when I say what comes out of my mouth next.

"You did your best, and we can figure anything out together—can't we?" I place my hands on the pod as he passes it to me.

But as my hands touch the incubator, something inside whirls.

"I'm going to let go. I think your proximity is causing this reaction." He allows me to accept the full weight of the orb. Drohako steps behind me, his arms shooting protectively over my stomach.

The whirling piece of tech changes shape, the panels of its exterior shifting until it's no longer round. Pass-through portions appear on either side of the main sphere.

What I hold in my hands now almost appears to be a metal chastity belt in shape. Two leg holes have materialized from the sides while the bulk of the pod remains between the openings.

"Do I step in?" I wonder aloud.

"I will try it first to make sure it won't hurt

you," Drohako says nobly as he reaches around me, but I bat his hand away.

"No, no. I think it's okay. The brochure for spawning season made it seem like this would be a piece of cake, right? And I don't think those big gams of yours would fit," I say, knowing full well that the opening as provided would have a hard time making it over his calves.

"I will be right here," he whispers in my ear as I lift my foot into the leg hole.

Although my stance is wide, my legs fit perfectly into the pod pants opening.

As I acclimate to the feeling of metal contacting my skin, I recline onto his chest, trying to get a good view of what might be going on between my legs.

"I wonder if we need to press some hidden button—"

My words are cut short as spoken instructions emanate from between my thighs.

"Subject with matching DNA docked." The pod blinks three times before continuing. "Subject, be advised that you will feel a small pinch as the cocktail of pain and relaxation meds are administered."

Pain meds, that's a good sign, right?

I can't help but tense as I wait for the needle. At first, I'm stupidly curious about where the injection might be administered, but then I realize that if the pod is strapped between my legs, it's only got one place it can go.

"Do you think it will hurt?" The words rush out as I ask my mate, my chest tightening.

"I hope it does not." He moves his hands up to my chest, cupping my breasts in a way that could feel sexual, but one I only find comforting in this moment. "No matter what, I am here, mate."

I turn my head, maybe to kiss him, or maybe just to reassure myself that he's really there when I first feel it.

Something cool, but slick, as if it's already lubricated, is nudging gently at my entrance. Inadvertently, I clench my interior muscles and the probe pauses.

"Remain calm," the pod's robotic voice barks.

Drohako's hands squeeze gently again.

"Calm mate," he whispers into my ear before sucking my earlobe between his lips. The tingling of the nerves there shoots straight to my core and has me pushing down onto the probe without intending to.

I don't know if it should feel good, and I feel a little ashamed when a moan slips out of my mouth as the smooth rod slips deeper.

"Calm, perfect, and willing to bear my young," his voice groans behind me, and I feel the bulge under his loincloth hardening against my back.

Should I feel bad about being turned on by this?

The way Drohako is tugging at my nipples now tells me he doesn't care—so why should I?

I can ignore the fear if I focus on the pleasure, at least. Orgasmic childbirth is like a hippie human thing too, right? I try to pull up memories from old station satellite transmissions of Earth documentaries—but there's no room in my mind to ignore what's currently happening between my legs.

The probe vibrates slowly, testing my depth. It slides a few inches deeper before stuttering and withdrawing. The metal shaft repeats these actions twice before going deeper each time.

All the while, Drohako is kneading my breasts, running his tongue up and down the column of my neck in what I suppose the barbarian version of comfort is.

My pussy is drenching itself over the cool metallic rod, as I can only assume it calibrates itself inside me.

I'm lost to the sensations until the probe bottoms out at my cervix.

Drohako is muttering something filthy in my ear when I feel something that's definitely less of a pinch and more of a jab.

White flashes before my eyes and my muscles bunch as my back arches, stupidly attempting to get away from something that's strapped to my body.

"Mate?" Drohako asks as he holds me tight.

I shut my eyes, the sharp pain only lasting a few seconds before shifting into something else entirely.

"Oh!" I bellow as the stabbing feeling ebbs into a dull ache. I gasp again as that sensation morphs into a throbbing release.

"Are you alright?" His gruff voice behind me questions.

"I..I..." I can't make the words come out right as the blood is drawn from my brain down to my sex.

There's not a single iota of pain left when my pussy first spasms, as if whatever injection they've given me has induced one of the most intense and instantaneous orgasms of my entire life.

I'm a trembling mess as I desperately clutch his forearms. Pleasure waves surge through me, overwhelming and unstoppable.

"Mate?" Drohako holds me ever tighter as he begs for a reply.

The only response I can give him is a primal growl emanating from deep within my throat. Through the crashing nebulas of ecstasy, I can barely feel the probe as it presses deeper.

Childbirth should hurt, shouldn't it? My mind wanders as my surroundings become unclear.

I clench my legs shut as tightly as possible, trying to hold on as my body is lifted higher.

I enter a state of blissful transcendence as my orgasm overwhelms me. Every nerve in my body explodes with sparking joy and my mind drifts blindly into euphoria. With each pleasurable contraction, my clit bobs with increasing intensity.

This shouldn't feel good. I try to make sense of the confusion, my mind working overtime to find a rational explanation.

Even through my haze, I hear what sounds like suction. "...don't worry, I have you..." Drohako sounds far away.

I reach up, hoping to find him. My searching fingers bury into the coarseness of his beard. It's something to ground me, and I hold on for dear life.

The only thing I can perceive for minutes is the feeling of his facial hair. I'm probably clinging to it tightly, but I refuse to give up my one hold on reality. My psyche refuses to free itself entirely from the world.

"... mate?" His voice sounds like it's down some long hallway.

I lose my grip on him, and with my grip goes my last shred of consciousness.

I jolt back, a sizzle running down my spine.

"... I'm here..." he says, the voice getting closer. "Breathe for me." His voice is suddenly booming.

Like a good submissive, I follow his command,

drawing a breath through my nostrils, feeling my chest expand.

His hands are still on me, rising as my lungs fill with air.

"I'm okay," I croak. I'm conscious, but whatever has just happened has left my bones feeling as though they've been replaced with jelly.

"I think you had a seizure," he whispers in my ear, laying me down onto a familiar soft fur.

The feeling returns to my limbs as they connect to the hair-covered surface beneath me. My wet thighs press together.

"No, not that," I groan, attempting to push myself up to my elbows. I feel...*fine,* surprisingly. There's no lingering pain, and I'm left feeling delightfully used.

When I look down, all I see is my swollen mound.

"Where's the pod?"

"Safe," he says, checking me over. He opens my thighs and looks at my pussy before gazing up at me again.

"Was it painful?" he asks, a slight lilt to his tone, as if he almost doesn't want to know.

"Only for a moment, after that I...well, I *came*." No point in hiding it.

"Is that normal for human childbirth?" He seems amused.

"Decidedly not."

"Well, we'll consider it an improvement, then." He looks at me as I open my mouth to ask the question he already knows I want the answer to. "Our child is safe, resting now in the pod."

He tenderly supports me by placing one hand under my rump and cradling me with the other under my shoulder. He guides me back over to the rocky outcropping on the cave wall where the pod had initially been placed.

Our child sits comfortably, nestled in a cozy nest of furs. As I gaze at the purple fetus, I notice it's suspended in a liquid that looks uncannily like molten lava, a stark contrast to anything I could ever conceive as coming from my own body.

Bizarre, I mouth, reaching my hand up to the thing that was nestled inside me just moments ago.

"What should we call him?" I crane my neck back up to the face of my alien.

His eyes flash with some realization. "What's *your* name, mate?"

The ease with which I accepted "mate" in place of my own name shows a longing for submission that surpasses my need for individuality. Belonging to Drohako is almost more important than some silly little detail.

"What's my name?" I ask curiously. The letters of it swirl into place inside my mind. "Isn't it curious how nothing else seems to hold any importance as long as I'm in your possession?" With a smile, I reach out and place my hand on the window of the pod, relishing in the comforting warmth that spreads through my fingers.

"What should I call you?" he asks, almost as if he's granting me permission to be something beyond his. "You, my mate, are the pillar of strength that sustains our bloodline. Our son must know your name to praise his lineage."

Through my submission to an alien barbarian, I've tapped into a strength as mighty as a Volkroth—a warrior, a mother.

I smile, searching his expectant face.

"My name is—"

ABOUT THE AUTHOR

www.petrapalerno.com

Petra Palerno is a lifelong weirdo who loves writing otherworldy romance and erotica. If it's got any combination of aliens, fae, or other assorted monsters count her in. She lives in the Midwest with her husband and a menagerie of spoiled pets. She can often be seen making a cocktail at her in-home tiki bar and lurching away into her writer's cave like the true goblin she is.

www.patreon.com/petrapalerno

If you enjoyed this story, you'll probably love my patreon. There you'll find serials, spicy art, behind the scenes looks into my writing process, and patreon exclusive special editions. Even my free level subscribers get a weekly smutty serial!

 instagram.com/petrapalerno

tiktok.com/@petrapalerno

 x.com/petrapalerno

facebook.com/petrapalerno

ALSO BY PETRA

All I Wanted Was Sushi But I Got Abducted By Aliens Instead: Bubble Babes #1

2023

All I Wanted Was To Become A Scientist But Now I've Got An Alien Boyfriend: Bubble Babes #2

2023

All I Wanted Was a Glass of Vino but an Alien Duke Kidnapped Me Instead: Bubble Babes #3

2023

Love On The Korlyan Moon

2024

COMING SOON

All I Wanted Was to Read Books but I Became a Space Pirate Instead: Bubble Babes #4

ESTIMATED PUBLICATION 2024

Soldiers Of Sontafrul 6 #1

ESTIMATED PUBLICATION 2025